Praise fo,

A dark and wonderful novel, ... details, herbal lore, traditions and s. ...s. Steadman's clear-eyed storytelling and colourful period voice give life to a vibrant cast of characters drawn against the backdrop of tragic historical events.

— LOUISA MORGAN, A SECRET HISTORY
OF WITCHES

Infused as it is with aromas of rosemary, fennel and lavender, even the healers' herbs do not mask the reek of the injustice that sits at the heart of *Widdershins*. Powerful and shocking.

— WYL MENMUIR, THE MANY

This meticulously researched account of a bigoted man's inhumanity to women in the seventeenth century will make the modern reader grateful to have been born in an enlightened age.

— MARI GRIFFITH, THE WITCH OF EYE

Helen's writing has a persuasive and empathetic force, weaving together historical fact with modern concerns about the treatment of women.

— HELEN MARSHALL, THE MIGRATION

A compelling and nuanced account of the clash of cultures that claimed so many lives. Steadman's carefully interwoven narrative conjures a world of herbal lore, folk practice and belief and convincingly portrays the psychological and ideological forces that form a perpetrator, and the social structures that sustain him.

— HELEN LYNCH, THE ELEPHANT AND
THE POLISH QUESTION

There are plenty of books, both fact and fiction, available about the witch-trial era, but not only did I not know about such trials in Newcastle, I have not read a novel that so painstakingly and vividly evokes both the fear and joy of living at that time.

— SALLY ZIGMUND, HISTORICAL NOVEL
SOCIETY

Helen Steadman knows her subject inside out and gives great insight into a period of history that we should feel ashamed of. Two very different narrators bring us careering towards the horrifying denouement.

— FIN GRAY, DUPLICITY

In the witchfinder John Sharpe, Steadman has given us a religious psychopath par excellence, a deeply conflicted man for whom cognitive dissonance could have been invented, filled to overflowing with impotent rage for his immaculately damaged childhood.

— TED CURTIS, THE DARKENING LIGHT

SOLSTICE

SOLSTICE
NEWCASTLE WITCH TRIALS
BOOK III

HELEN STEADMAN

First published by Bell Jar Books, London, 2023

British Library Cataloguing in Publication Data
A catalogue record for this book is available
from the British Library.

ISBN: 9781915421975

Developmental Editor: Julian Webb
Cover Designer: Ollie Eskriett, Move Design
Illustrator: Chess Heward Art

This fictional work is for entertainment only.
Do not try any recipe, procedure or prescription in this book.

For My Children

Contents

But I was like a gentle lamb led to the slaughter
And I did not know they had devised plots against me

Jeremiah 11:19, *NIV*

Solstice: 'One or other of the two times in the year, midway
between the two equinoxes, when the sun, having reached
the tropical points, is farthest from the equator and appears
to stand still. A turning, culminating, or stopping point; a
furthest limit; a crisis. A standing still (of the sun).'

Oxford English Dictionary

SPRING

Witch Cottage

ROSE

Outside, in a night that should be populated by none other than foxes, badgers and owls, there were others abroad. The length of the valley, women were rumoured to assemble after dark to gossip and plot, and it seemed their number included my stepmother, May Driver. I slid from bed and opened the chamber door a crack to see her winding that luxurious golden braid of hers into a coif and shrugging on her cloak. Out she sidled in her stocking feet, carrying a pair of clogs in her right hand and my late mother's leather satchel in her left. She was no midwife, not like my mother and grandmother before her, so had no cause to be out at this hour. A lover, perhaps? Would she betray my father? He could be a difficult man, even I understood that, and there'd been the usual terrible argument this morning, but he'd put a roof over May and her sister's heads and spared them from their wicked father all these years.

Once she'd cleared the house, I crept to the window and raised the curtain to watch her progress along the crisp, white path. After tiptoeing past the barn, she slid her feet into her clogs and followed the river into the woods, with only the moon for company. Apart from me, the household was dead to the world, so I put on my cloak and boots and

3

slipped out behind her. The frozen river meant no rushing water to deaden my following footsteps. I planted each foot carefully, mindful of every crack and creak, not wanting to disturb May, a woman so skittish that she flinched if Da so much as raised a hand to scratch his ear.

She hastened onwards, occasionally stopping to peer over her shoulder. Veiled with a hood, my face would be little more than a shadow to her. Believing herself alone, she walked at a good pace, making it easy to follow her noisy footsteps. When a barn owl screeched, May started and crashed through the undergrowth until she tripped and fell. After some cursing, she scrambled to her feet and limped along the deer paths hidden beneath the canopy of bare branches. Now I knew her destination. It would be interesting to learn what had fetched a married woman to Witch Cottage at midnight. The deserted house rested in a clearing and had made the perfect childhood hideaway to play my favourite game with Tilly and Henry Green. The idea for it had come to me in a dream, but it wasn't something we could get up to under Granny's eye.

I stumbled on the cottage by accident as a child when my pet ewe ran off, with me in pursuit. Although a sound enough dwelling, it stood empty, yet despite being in the heart of the woods, it showed no signs of being overgrown. By rights, woodbines should have throttled the place, elder should have pushed in through the floor and out through the roof, and mice should have nested in the rafters. A cottage so kempt meant someone was keeping nature at bay, but I had no idea who, or why. Inside, the only room contained rough wooden furniture: a bed, a table, a settle and a cracket beside the hearth. Crooked shelves stacked with hundreds of jars and crocks lined the walls. As children, we'd used the three-legged cracket to balance on while we lifted down jars, running our fingertips over dried brown clumps and cobwebby residues. Crowing over our treasure, we'd puzzled over the secret apothecary.

Later, when we asked my grandmother about our discovery, her mouth pursed until it resembled a cat's backside. It took a while to draw the tale from her, but she told us the shack had belonged to an old crone, the green woman in Mutton Clog, who'd spent her days trading both herbs and ancient wisdom. According to Granny, *green woman* was no more than an innocent-sounding name for a witch and that explained why nobody lived in the cottage. People in these parts were superstitious and feared their own shadows, but the thought of witches thrilled us and we clutched each other, shuddering in delight.

'Never set foot in Witch Cottage again,' said my grandmother. 'And pray your da doesn't get wind of it, Rosie, else he'll knock you into the middle of next week. The three of you. Do you hear?'

But we did go back, stealing away from our errands whenever we could. One day, we were playing the secret game and Tilly lay on the earthen floor, my poppet hidden beneath her pinny. Henry crept up and plucked Dolly from her hiding place, carried her to the table, and drew a stick across her throat. I snatched the stick and ran him through with it, and he obediently collapsed. Afterwards, Henry and Tilly changed places and we started afresh. Though they were both older than me, no matter how often we played, I was always the saviour.

So intent were we on our amusement that we were startled when May burst through the door in time to catch me running Tilly through with the imaginary blade. My stepmother stood in the doorway, hands on hips, while her younger siblings shrank under her stare.

'What are you lot up to?'

My heart raced and I bit my lip, unable to explain the nature of my game.

'We're not up to anything, May, but please don't tell Granny you found us in Witch Cottage.'

'You haven't swallowed any berries from those jars have you?'

'No, they're not ours. We'd never steal.'

At this, her face softened. 'I didn't mean that, hinny, but some of those crocks contain poison, so they want hoyed out.'

'But we love to look at them and we promise not to take any and not all of them are dangerous.' I held up an earthenware jar that housed the skeletons of brittle leaves and breathed in the faint scent. 'They smell of the milk puddings we have in summer. Bayleaf.'

'Aye, your Granny's spiced posset. Go on, the three of you, get yourselves home before you're missed. The jars can stay but not their contents. I should've emptied them out long ago.' She removed some crocks and pots from the shelves and began stacking them on the table. 'And stop calling it Witch Cottage. Meg Wetherby lived here and she was no witch. She was very dear to your mother, Rose, and she was like a grandmother to Tom Verger. He looks after this place in her memory, so keep it tidy.'

Ashamed of our mockery, we nodded solemnly and set off home. Once out of May's sight and hearing, I made my friends swear not to mention what we'd been doing, either to their da, or mine. If our fathers heard about my game, they'd forbid us from playing it again, so it would just have to have to be another secret we kept, along with Witch Cottage.

The Sins of the Mother

PATIENCE

Father had carried out his ministry in some godforsaken places in the past, but none more so than the hilly parish of Mutton Clog. It must have gone midnight, but the place would not be greatly improved by daylight. Hand on heart, I could not say it pleased any member of the Leaton family to be ousted from the Diocese of Ely and sent north to Durham. Not me, not my twin brother Earnest and certainly not our father. None of us relished the notion of living amongst the poor and the ignorant, but in the circumstances, we counted ourselves fortunate that Father had been given a new benefice.

Judging by the dearth of dwellings, our new situation comprised a meagre scattering of inhabitants. Ostensibly, Father was here to provide the necessary discipline to a parish gone to seed. But really, this northern outpost served as a humiliating and public punishment for the terrible shame that had – through no fault of his – cast its shadow on our family. Neither had his children escaped opprobrium, with my social standing destroyed and my brother's vocation finished before it started.

No one could blame our former archdeacon for any of this as he found himself in an untenable position.

Conveniently for us, the late Reverend Foster bequeathed a living in the parish of Mutton Clog that not another priest in England wanted. Our archdeacon took great pains to convince my father that this forgotten corner of the country all but cried out for his particular brand of Christianity. That venerable man should have saved his breath. Whatever his reasoning, it made little difference. Here we were, like it or not, because my father currently held such a low status in the eyes of the Church that he was in no position to argue.

Our family's fall from grace had not been immediately apparent to the cathedral authorities, but our congregants soon started tattling during Father's sermons. How soon those upright people forgot they should open their mouths in God's praise, or not at all. But the scurrilous gossipmongers refused to be silenced and once the rumours reached the ears of the archdeacon, he was compelled to act. Despite losing his marriage, his livelihood, his home and his reputation, Father refused to discuss the matter with me and more than once instructed me to hold my tongue. This left me no option but to consult our garrulous cook to assuage my sinful curiosity on the matter. And so, courtesy of my mother's uncontrollable loins, we were compelled to give up our decent living in Ely and venture to this remote dale.

Our pilgrimage north was protracted and uncomfortable but not otherwise offensive until we were within a few miles of our journey's end, where the frost thickened to ice and then to snow, slowing our progress because the horses' hooves could find no purchase as they hauled us up the long incline from Durham. The driver insisted on going at the slowest pace possible, afraid one of his horses would slip and break a leg.

Close to midnight, and not too far from our destination, we arrived at the brow of a steep valley, quilted in white. The driver refused the descent, protesting about the deep snow, arguing the case for his horses' welfare and never mind ours. Father and Earnest got into an argument with the man, who was not easily cowed, and additionally in possession of a whip. Forced to admit defeat, we dismounted and my menfolk unloaded our belongings from the wagon. Our luggage was modest, otherwise we would have had to discard it. Before abandoning us, the driver pointed in the vague direction of a small hill, half a mile shy of the valley floor, where we could see the outline of a small church and a large manse.

The dale looked deceptively pure. Below us, gleaming in the moonlight, lay the silver curve of a frozen river, a handful of humble cottages and a few farmhouses. Otherwise, the hills and vales were given over to woodland and pasture. At the very least, it presented an invigorating change from the hot stench of Ely marketplace with its constant press of so many unsanitary bodies.

During the final part of our journey, I lost count of the number of slips and trips. It was a disgrace, arriving in our new parish at the dead of night, carrying our own chattels, covered in snow and who knew what else besides. After retracing our steps a few times, we found our way – in spite of, rather than because of – the wagon driver, whose directions and descriptions left a lot to be desired. If not for the moon, we would still be wandering the hills or more likely frozen to death on them.

At the lych gate, Father left his baggage and walked towards his new church, skirting the ill-aligned gravestones as he went. He paused at his predecessor's grave and knelt in the snow to pray. Reputedly, the Reverend Foster was so slipshod he was barely deserving of the honorific and should have been defrocked. Instead, the priest was buried in the graveyard, albeit in the shade of the gravedigger's hut. In the grey light of the moon, I could see that beneath the snow the mound of clay covering his grave had not yet settled. His resting place was marked with a wooden cross and from it hung a pagan wreath of holly and ivy. Much loved, then, the old priest, despite his derelict habits, which told me everything I needed to know about the spiritual poverty of our parishioners. The whole dale stank of rebellion. This is what came from living in the middle of nowhere and lacking a firm hand to guide the inhabitants in the true path of righteousness. I looked forwards to taking them to task and bringing them back to the Lord. Anyone failing to meet the required standard would have to throw himself on the mercy of the Leaton family, which was a quality often in short supply.

Father finished praying and walked to the church. He would want privacy there, so Earnest and I carried our belongings to the manse. Almost larger than the church, our new home consisted of two storeys and an attic with a steeply pitched slate roof, whose ridge was on par with the church bellcote. Crow-stepped gables flanked each side, and in the roof a garret window protruded. Built from the same golden stone as the church, the manse glittered with windows leaded into diamonds, each pane trapping the moonlight, creating an illusion of the whole house blazing with an argentine fire. Those panes would require some polishing but this task would not fall to me when more pressing matters would impinge upon my time. I had no intention of frittering away my life on matters domestic.

Inside, we heaped everything onto the floor. Never in all my born days had I been so exhausted or so cold. The fens of home were almost unbearable in winter, but nothing could have prepared me for the frigidity of this far-flung place. The further north from Durham we climbed, the lower the temperature fell and the deeper the snow became. The last leg of our journey had almost reduced me to tears, and I was not given to crying. At home in Ely, spring was in full bloom, getting ready for summer, unlike Mutton Clog, which was still trying to shrug off the final days of winter.

My brother located some prickets and lit the beeswax candles, enabling us to take in our opulent surroundings. A broad staircase and its handsome banisters curved out of sight to the next storey. Above our heads a cornice ran around the ceiling and beneath our feet was a colourful tiled mosaic, half-covered with a silken rug. To the side stood a polished table that served no useful purpose. Several doors led off the hall, each carved and bearing a brass knob. There was an aversion here to whatever was plain and ordinary, and I dreaded to see what lay beyond each door. If only we were back in our small and simple former home, lit with humble tallow candles and rushlights.

'Earnest, do you think we will ever be forgiven and admitted to Ely again? Might the archdeacon allow us back?'

'Doubtful. Maybe in a decade or two, assuming memories fade, but if I were you, Patience, I would get used to living here.'

'Easy for you to say when you have but a matter of months to put up with the place.'

'Ah, yes,' he sneered. 'The easy way out. A life of luxury at sea instead of the hardship of blessing fat infants and planning my wedding to the daughter of a wealthy landowner.'

I envied him his prospects, however diminished, since ministry was a path denied to me, with marriage my only prospect. A thin band of gold was insufficient recompense for a life of marital servitude so I had no plans to marry or have children.

My brother would embark in a few short months on a voyage as naval chaplain and need only reside here until he learnt the name of his ship. Arguably, he was most affected by my mother's exploits. Newly ordained, he was due to receive a stipend in a thriving parish. Betrothed to his patron's daughter, all that remained was to serve a few blameless years as curate, and once the elderly incumbent passed, Earnest would marry, step up as vicar and preside over a flourishing parish.

Immediately the scandal had emerged, my brother lost

both his stipend and his betrothed. My father lost his living and counted himself blessed not to be flung out of the ministry altogether. Our archdeacon had sympathised, given Father's decades of blameless service, but the diocese could no longer accommodate him, and the neighbouring dioceses were likewise reluctant. Just when all seemed desperate, the benefice in Mutton Clog fell vacant following the demise of the Reverend Foster, celebrant here for over half a century.

I took one of the prickets. 'Fetch those bags upstairs, Earnest, so we can unpack and get to sleep because it will be an early start in the morning.'

Grumbling, he thrust my valise under one oxter, picked up the other two and stamped up the stairs behind me.

❧

The manse was so ornate it bordered on papish when all that we required were a few plain rooms and some honest wood furniture. Our Lord espoused poverty, simple fare and basic clothing. These luxurious trappings made me wonder whether the Reverend Foster hadn't been a Catholic priest, secretly practising forbidden rites. Left to my own devices, I would raze this manse to the ground and build in its place a more humble abode, something akin to our former home.

Father was also appalled by our sybaritic surroundings, and especially so by the main bedchamber. Yet another silk rug covered the wooden floor, and a huge bedstead dominated the room. Its head and footboards were carved with seafaring adventures, with each of its four posts decorated in the same style. Upholstered with brocade curtains, a feather tick and a tasselled bolster, it was a bed fit for a pope.

'By rights,' said Father, 'we should consign this lot to the flames. No decent man of God should lie in such trappings.'

He ran a finger over the dark wood and perched on the bed. 'Although, it is harder than it looks, so it may be possible to sleep here without it weighing too heavily on my conscience, and as any virtuous Christian will tell you, waste is worse than luxury. Perhaps I should compensate by not drawing its curtains against the chill, though I can't recall a colder Easter.'

This manse worried me. Any occupant of such a grandiose building would be in danger of seeing himself as higher and mightier than God. We would need to take great care to guard our souls against extravagance whilst we lived here, which I had already decided would not be for long. Somehow, I would restore our family's reputation so we could return to the Isle of Ely, if not in glory, then at least without shame.

The Barrener

ROSE

A good hour had passed while I stood outside Witch Cottage in the wintry wood. Nobody had come near, or I'd have heard them approaching long before they sighted me. So unless May's secret lover was already awaiting her arrival, no tryst was underway. There'd been no noise from the dwelling beyond the scraping sounds of a fire being laid, and when smoke wafted from the chimney, I no longer cared if she was alone. The thought of a warm fire lured me out of my hiding place. I eased open the latch and slipped inside, closing the door carefully behind me, but not carefully enough. I disturbed May, who was all alone, a dark silhouette outlined by the firelight, hunched over a boiling crock, ladle at the ready. At the sound of the door opening, she jumped and dropped the ladle into the pot.

'Rose!' she said, 'what are you doing here in the middle of the night?'

'I might ask you the same question. What are you doing creeping about the woods alone at this hour? Are you betraying my father?'

'I'm betraying no one,' said May. 'On my soul. But please go home in case you're missed, lass. In case we're both missed.'

If she wasn't betraying my father, then why did she look so guilty? The dense air was perfumed with a muddle of herbs reminiscent of Granny's pantry. The cloves she studded our hams with. The juniper berries she added to our Christmas puddings. The spearmint she mixed with vinegar, salt and sugar to flavour our potatoes. Only, these weren't the friendly smells of my grandmother's kitchen, but something darker, more pungent and bitter. I plucked the ladle from the pot, poured its contents from a height and watched the inky liquid suck in the firelight. This horrible potion wasn't anything I'd seen either here or at home.

'What's this? What are you brewing here at midnight?'

My stepmother didn't answer me, but took the ladle from my hand and lifted the boiling pot onto a trivet.

There could be only one answer. I thought back to the argument that morning. Of my father's accusations. Of the many arguments down the years. Of his demands. Of the various visits to the physic. Of the threats to throw May out, and with her, Tilly. His lack of sons was Da's favourite topic for the table, and he could not get past the notion of a houseful of lads cast in his own image.

'I only married her so she could give me a string of fat bairns,' he said to Granny as if his goodwife wasn't present. 'If a farm is to survive, it needs bairns, and lads more so. It's proven that I can create a lad.' A nerve twitched high on May's cheek, and he narrowed sly eyes at her. 'And so can she if the mart gossip holds water.'

Crimson mottled May's neck and breast, but she stayed silent during his tirade.

'You know what farmers do when they find themselves lumbered with a barrener, don't you?' Da grinned and ran a forefinger across his throat.

'Andrew,' said Granny, an edge of warning in her voice.

My stomach clenched so I pushed my plate away. As a bairn, I'd had countless fights with Da over ewes that couldn't produce lambs. He'd let me keep Giddy as a pet but the years soon crept up on her. First a barrener and then a gummer, she'd struggled to eat the coarse moorland grass and had to be kept in a valley paddock, along with a few other gummers for company. There, they ate soft grass and expensive fodder. Their lambing days were behind them but I couldn't bear to see them slaughtered. They had naught to give but their affection and their lovely wool, which spared them, but Da resented ewes eating precious pasture and winter feed when they'd have no lambs to show for it. I loved Giddy and Da loved me so he indulged me, but I had less faith in whether he loved his second goodwife and worried what might become of her and her sister.

Every month, the tension in the house would build. Da needled May about her lack of issue at each new moon as she reached for the wooden box of clean rags, head bowed in apology, so we all guessed she was bleeding. It had been more than a moon since she last removed the box from the shelf – only a day or two over – but it wouldn't take Da long to notice. That morning, when May finally escaped Da's close scrutiny by clearing the table and carrying everything to the scullery, I got up to follow her.

'Sit down, Rose,' said Da. 'You're no servant.'

'May's no servant either,' I said, hurrying after her.

There were rumours that Da had bastards scattered throughout the dales, so he needed no remedy, but there were plants my stepmother could take to help her conceive. The mart wives often proffered tips for making my ewes fertile. Granny frowned on the use of herbs for anything other than flavouring her puddings and stews though, so I'd kept this knowledge to myself.

Once we were side by side, scraping the platters clean, I shared the secret with my stepmother.

'There are remedies,' I whispered. 'Powders and tinctures. Just a few drops in your morning milk. The mart wives have lots of tricks for getting ewes into lamb. They say red clover would help you get a bairn and they know the best phase of the moon for tupping to get a ram – a son, if you like.'

She didn't turn but touched my wrist. 'The mart wives have told me much the same. Thank you, pet, but I'm beyond anyone's help.'

But it seemed May had heeded the mart wives' advice, after all, because here she was in Witch Cottage. Given Granny's dislike of using plants for anything other than eating, it wasn't surprising May was brewing here, rather than at home under Granny's long nose. But the hideous julep didn't look or smell anything like red clover.

'May, are you boiling up herbs to help you conceive? Because if you are, there's no need to do it here at midnight. You could use my shepherd's hut. No one goes there till the lambing, so you've got a few days, and I won't tell a soul.'

'Thank you, Rose, but I'm not trying to procure a baby. Conceiving children isn't difficult for me, sadly. I'm already with child and that's the problem. I have to get rid of it before your Da finds out or he'll keep me prisoner till I give birth.'

I gaped at May, and it was hard to say whether I was more shocked at what she was doing to my father, or that she'd speak so badly of him. He was desperate for a son, but I couldn't imagine he'd treat his goodwife so cruelly in the attempt. May picked up a small bowl and ladled the dark decoction into it, wafting her hand back and forth in the rising steam to cool it down. Whatever was in that bowl was not intended to create a child but to take one away. My loyalties were torn – my stepmother was good to me and I loved her, but Da was in need of a son and had been for as long as I could remember. Even now, May might be carrying a lad, so why destroy him? I knew the answer, of course. She didn't want a child for the same reason I didn't want a child.

And I knew just where she'd learnt to make this decoction. Not from the mart wives but from her closest friend, my own mother. She was a midwife and must have taught May. Midwifery wasn't just about helping babies into the world but also helping them out of it. I already knew this thanks to the mart wives. Little went on in Mutton Clog that they didn't repeat to me when Granny's back was turned.

'Aren't you worried about being caught, May? You need to be careful. I found you so somebody else could stumble on you here just as easily.'

'I'm not a bit worried,' she said. 'I'm doing naught wrong. All I'm doing is restoring my menses. The law permits it, providing there's been no quickening.'

Poor May, having to hide behind what might or might not be permitted under the law. I was ignorant of such matters and suspected that so was she, but whatever the rights and wrongs of her deeds, Da would judge it one way. That May was killing his sons. It would be the finish of her if he found out and he'd throw my stepmother out of the house and her sister with her. Da wasn't my only concern, though. When Granny and May's backs were turned, the mart wives had also filled my ears with tales about my Grandmother Chandler. That she was hanged as a witch. That my mother was tried as well and narrowly avoided the hangman's noose. That they were both accused of killing infants before they were born.

So May was running a terrible risk, and in Witch Cottage of all places. Using herbs to destroy an unborn child was dangerous, but I couldn't blame anyone for it. Just the thought of birthing made me shiver. My mother died in childbed, and my newborn brother with her, so I'd grown up with a dread of dying the same way. Time and again, I'd wished that my mother had chosen her own life over my brother's. She'd had the means to end her second pregnancy, and had she done so, she'd be alive and well today. Instead, I'd grown up with a terror of childbirth and resolved to avoid it. I was of marrying age but had no intention of giving up my life for a child, so why should my stepmother?

'May, are you afraid of dying in childbed like my mother? Is that why you do this?'

'No, hinny. That's not it. Here, let me show you.'

She removed her pinny and laid it on the settle, unfastened her bodice and unhooked her kirtle. Then she took off her shift and stood in her coif, stockings, garters and clogs.

In the flickering firelight, my stepmother's milky skin shimmered with purple, green and yellow. At first, I refused to believe what she was showing me, preferring to believe her clumsy, always walking into walls or catching herself on sharp corners. But these beautiful colours clearly mapped my father's cruelty, so I could no longer deny it.

'Rose, if there was any other way, I wouldn't have you learn this about your da. You love him,' said May, 'but he has a darkness in him.'

Da was raining blows on the body of the woman who'd raised me. He'd always had a temper, but this handiwork wasn't done in temper because the bruising had a careful pattern to it, with no marks visible beyond neckline, cuff or hem.

'How long has he been hitting you?' I asked, holding her hands.

'More or less from the minute the ring went on my finger and there was no way of turning back.' She paused. 'He blames me for not being your mother and tells me I bring it all on myself. But none of this is my fault.'

I let go of her hands and hoped she'd cover herself. The sight of her made me feel ashamed for being so innocent all these years. Worse than innocent – ignorant. Those muffled sounds from their chamber. Always worse in the mornings. Granny got on with her work, bossing me and Tilly about as if all were well and neither of us questioned it. But it was clear to me now. My stepmother didn't want to bear another child forced on her.

'Does he take you against your will?'

May didn't reply and had no need to when the answer was written in her eyes and across her hide.

'It would be easy enough for me to interrupt,' I said. 'To bang on the door and ask Da whether he wants porridge or bacon to break his fast.'

'It won't stop him and it'll anger him more. Naught can save me from him. Naught. Do as your granny does and keep out of it and just let me get it over with as quickly as possible.'

She couldn't bring herself to look at me. How bad her childhood home must have been that she'd willingly left it to marry Da, where her only reward was a life lived in constant fear.

'I won't breathe a word but please be careful sneaking out in the night. I woke up and followed you. It could just as easily have been Da. And the mart wives' tongues are always wagging the length and breadth of the dale.' I drew her into my arms. This woman who'd been a mother to me for most of my life, who refused to carry her husband's child, and no wonder. 'Can you leave him?' I asked.

'Can I escape from him, you mean?' She scoffed and her reaction made me feel very young. 'I've nowhere to go, except my father's house, and Tilly with me. And what sort of life would we have there? Don't make me say it out loud, lass.'

May moved into the farmhouse when I was still a bairn, and so did her younger sister, with no explanation. I never questioned it at the time, excited to have my friend living with us, but of course the mart wives had put me right a few years back. Poor Tilly. Poor May. And poor Henry Green, passed off as their brother. I regretted my mistrust of her, blundering into the cottage with my accusations when my stepmother had endured so much in her early life and now had to endure my father.

'Could you run away with someone kind like Tom Verger?'

'Tom Verger?' She gave a bitter laugh. 'Your da would sooner see me in the ground than see me with him. Besides, Tom only ever loved one lass and she's... she's long gone.'

All too easy for me to tell a trapped woman to leave, because I struggled to understand why anyone would stay. Although we shared a roof and a family, how very different our lives were. It was unfair to suggest it, when she was more scared of what would happen to her if she left than if she stayed. But I could advise her, so she wouldn't have to swallow these poisonous herbs.

'May, there's a safer way to spare yourself. Being near ewes in lamb can sometimes... restore the menses. Come and stay with me in the hut. The flock are due to yean in a week or so.'

'Aye, you're right, but your da is wise to that as well. Why else does he keep me away from the livestock? Please don't think your advice isn't appreciated, Rose, but I need to drink this, and quickly. Sorry.'

She picked up the cup and drank its contents, gagging all the time she swallowed. I picked up her clothes and smoothed them out. When she'd recovered from drinking her noxious potion, she dressed herself and I fastened her bodice and boots.

'Everyone in the dale knew what Andrew Driver was like, yet still I married him.'

The next question didn't bear asking, but it had to be asked.

'You knew what he was like because he did the same to my mother?'

Stupidly, I'd hoped that Da's violence had begun as a result of grief at my mother's death, as if that would somehow make it forgiveable. When May nodded, I saw the whole of my father. He'd never raised a hand to me, so I'd judged him to be a fair man, if a difficult one, closing my mind to certain sights and sounds for so many years.

She nodded. 'Everyone, including me, imagined what

Jane suffered but I gave in to him in spite of that. Had to, for Tilly's sake.' She stroked my face and tucked a tendril of hair behind my ear. You're so alike, you and Jane. I loved her, and she loved you very much.'

That was never in any doubt and neither was my father's love for my mother till today. I'd always supposed him grief-stricken, but a man so violent towards his goodwife could never truly grieve her.

'Your secret's safe with me, May, but doing this to yourself won't be doing you any good. Please try to get away. Perhaps someone in a distant dale would take you and Tilly in. The mart wives will know of someone and they'd say naught to Da.'

'Don't be so sure of that, Rose. The mart wives know just what they can and can't get away with saying when it comes to your da. Believe me, Andrew will never let me leave while there's breath in his body. I can stand this and I must until my sister finds either a husband or a live-in post, because I can no sooner leave her under your father's roof than I could leave her under my father's roof.'

A Secret

PATIENCE

The three of us walked to the gravedigger's hut and my father rapped on the door. The man who answered was red-haired and green-eyed, brash next to us dark and dour Leatons. His complexion was as ruddy as ours were pallid, which was to be expected for a man labouring in the elements. He was broad-shouldered and easily a head taller than Father and Earnest. His shape was not unpleasing, but I reminded myself that it resulted from digging graves for a living, and what could be heavier than a corpse whose soul had departed, or the clay it was due to rest in? Earnest and my father were more delicately built because they dedicated themselves to a higher purpose. In addition, the idle sexton looked too thoroughly nourished for a man in the keep of the church. Too well fed meant too well paid. Perhaps savings might be gleaned from that quarter in view of our small parish and its light workload. Before I could broach this with my father, he set off with the sexton to the church, where, after a few false starts, a peal broke the morning silence, sending the bellcote birds fleeing for quieter lodgings. If the Mutton Cloggers hoped to spend the sabbath toasting their toes by the fire, they had better think twice. The bell pealed through hill and dale, summoning the reluctant worshippers to Sunday observance. Without breaking his fast, Father would host a service immediately and show the parishioners how a church should be run.

After an unforgivable delay, the motley congregation eventually made their way through the drifts of snow. Once they were assembled, the bell ceased its pealing, and my brother and I followed them into our new church. Before the main door was a small gabled narthex that was barely longer than me and scarcely twice my breadth. Wide enough to carry in a coffin, it was fitted on its left-hand side with an oak bench. The wooden seat shone with use, proving that more parishioners cared to sit outside the church than in, which would soon change.

Ahead of us stood a heavy oak door, and we pushed through it into a cruciform church with a vaulted ceiling. Easily as overwrought as the manse, it was embellished with stained glass lancets and furnished in oak. Father was installed in the pulpit, and Earnest and I sat in the front pew, encouraged that no parishioner had usurped us by sitting there. Behind us, the door closed as the sexton took up his station to the rear, bearing the processional cross as if it were a weapon. Father leant on his pulpit, counting his parishioners. According to the parish register – easily the most poorly kept document I had ever seen – several were missing, but we would discover the names of the non-observers in the goodness of time.

'My name is Hector Leaton,' said Father, his breath fogging the air as he spoke, 'but you will address me and refer to me only as Minister Leaton. I do not want to hear my Christian name on the lips of any person here and neither will I accept any diminutive of it.'

This announcement caused grumblings amongst the congregants, and a muttering of 'Fancies himself too high and mighty for Heck.' How dare they think it acceptable to speak over their priest? They would learn the error of their ways after my father had sermonised for two or three hours.

Father's rhetoric was wasted on his low-bred flock, who variously shivered, shuffled and fidgeted during the entire sermon. Following a lesson on greed, my father ended by admonishing his congregation.

'Beneath the thick snow, this valley must be verdant because you are all so full in the face, with unfurrowed brows. You may toil in the fields, but how much toil is it really, to plant and sow and reap under God's eye on land that is blasphemously close to being a second Eden? But the fat of the land is not yours for the keeping and you must ensure the church receives its tithe.'

Before his shocked parishioners could react, he uttered the benediction and held up his right hand to prevent anyone from rising.

'No one is to leave until you have each stated your name and occupation, so I can establish who is here and who is not. My daughter will take the register. Patience, if you would, please?'

The sexton called out his name in a tone more resonant than my father's, proving that Thomas Verger thought himself superior to his vicar. Next was a family by the name of Green, comprising two parents and three grown sons. One Farmer Johnson, widowed and sons gone to neighbouring dales. Blenkinsop, a hefty fellow, who lived on the midpoint between two parishes and felt himself entitled to alternate between this church and its rival further along the river. And a smattering of Smiths, Wrights and Carters, with many restless infants amongst them. When everyone had given their names, I completed the register, passed it to my father and pointed out the absentees.

'So, we are missing the Drivers: Andrew, Elizabeth, May and Rose, with the addition of Matilda Green. Why does Matilda Green reside with the Drivers?' He addressed the Green family. 'I presume Matilda is one of your brood? And if so, why does she roost with the Drivers?'

Mr Green responded. 'Because our Tilly's an ungrateful wretch, just like her sister, May.'

During Green's unpleasant speech, his youngest son's ears pinked and his goodwife and the other two sons lowered their heads. So, May Driver, née Green, had taken her sister to the marital home. Not unheard of but curious all the same. I prepared to move on to the other missing party when my father interrupted.

'Where is my churchwarden?' Father pointed at Verger, who shifted his feet. 'In fact, *who* is my churchwarden?'

'Sir Jack used to hold the post,' said the sexton. 'But he came to a bad end in the New World. Him and his plant-hunter.'

Father breathed heavily through his nose. 'I did not ask who it used to be, but who it is now.'

'By rights, it's Ralph Maddison from Hole House. Yon side of the river but seldom seen in the quarter of late.'

'When did you last see him?'

The sexton rubbed a large hand across his beard as if this would somehow aid his thinking.

'I've not clapped eyes on the man in months. Years, mebbes. Lying low somewhere, most likely.'

What kind of warden had any need to lie low? How remiss of this Maddison fellow. Easy to see how the parish had decayed under the Reverend Foster's lax governance.

'As this Maddison man has effectively resigned by his continued absence,' said Father, 'we must elect another warden.' He peered around the church, and the parishioners slunk lower in their pews. Past experience told me that my father would choose the most reluctant candidate. His eye rested on the sexton. 'Verger, you can do double duty until Maddison shows his face again.'

'Always happy to serve, Minister Leaton,' said the sexton, 'but as I'm already employed by the church, it's mebbes not right for me to hold an elected post as well.'

'Yours will be a temporary appointment until Maddison

returns to the fold. Thomas Verger for churchwarden. All those in favour?'

The congregation, with the exception of the sexton, immediately raised their hands and there came an enthusiastic chorus of ayes.

'Then it is done. Verger, you can begin by fining the Drivers for non-observance of the sabbath, an offence I consider to be amongst the most grave. Patience, when did that family last appear in church?'

A study of the register revealed the Drivers had absented themselves from church for over two decades. Two decades! On further perusal, the register showed there were whole years when the entire parish had absented itself, particularly in sixteen-fifty and the succeeding years. Furthermore, the register showed no record of any fine ever being levied, let alone paid. If this was an accurate record, many corrupt souls would require saving, and after such a lengthy period of non-observance, the Drivers would have to sell everything they owned to honour a debt of such magnitude.

I wondered if our new archdeacon had any idea of the advanced state of the spiritual rot here. Still, the Leatons were determined to get back into the Church's good graces and there was no surer way than by filling its coffers. If all proceeded to plan, we could be tucked up in our old beds in Ely by Christmas. When I advised Father of the extent of the Drivers' non-attendance, his eyes widened.

'Impossible. No God-fearing person could fail to attend church for so long.' He stared at the sexton, who stared at his own enormous feet. 'Come, Verger, out with it. In God's house and under His eye, you are beholden to tell the truth.'

'I'd say the register is accurate,' he replied, 'but with sound reason.'

'There are no reasons for not attending church,' said my father, 'only excuses, and you will supply me with the details immediately.'

But Thomas Verger refused to be drawn on why the

Drivers had flouted the law, so he must be protecting a deep secret. My whole being pulsed with the possibility of unearthing it. Not to satisfy any petty curiosity, but to return the lost lambs to the fold and save their souls. If that was to the betterment of my family's position, then all to the good.

꿍

Once dressed, I opened the heavy velvet curtains in my chamber. The snow had not melted and more had fallen in the night. The blue sky and shining sun were both promising, though. For all its opulence, the manse was bitterly cold. My room had its own fireplace but it was useless without someone to set a fire. Following my intervention, we had lost our former housekeeper, and our ungrateful wretch of a cook elected to remain in Ely, claiming that moving north would deprive her children of their mother. As if anyone needed a mother. Mine had flown the coop, yet I thrived without her.

Downstairs, Father had overcome his initial disquiet at our ostentatious surroundings and I found him in an alcove that overlooked the hills to the west, ensconced in a comfortable chair and working at his new desk. Many of the previous incumbent's personal effects remained, including three sandglasses of varying sizes, each engraved with an image of the reaper, top and bottom. These tawdry baubles showed just how deeply the canker of greed had set in with the former parish priest. Without interrupting my parent, I gathered the sandglasses and tucked them out of sight in a sideboard. The first of many good deeds for the day. My second was to check whether my brother had yet accounted for the Drivers' debt. A small task, but if I knew Earnest, he would have set it aside in favour of almost any other activity. For someone destined for a life serving God, my brother struggled to apply himself and it astonished me that he had graduated, yet alone been ordained. To hear his fellows, my twin's university years were spent carousing – behaviour entirely at odds with that required of a man set for the ministry. Yet, despite his youthful indiscretion, my brother had been set to be curate in an excellent parish. All gone now, of course.

As expected, Earnest was not poring over the parish register and accounts. Instead, he was loitering in the churchyard and bothering the sexton, so I went to speak to him there. Our temporary churchwarden was unashamedly grubby and smeared with what must be grave dirt, and I wondered whether Father had given any thought to this when elevating him to his elected position. I arrived in time to hear my brother being ordered about like a working man.

'Here, lad,' said the sexton, 'make yourself useful and pass me that trowel.'

Earnest paused, but whether due to offence at the order or ignorance of the implement in question, I could not tell.

'Before the sun goes down, lad.'

Earnest bent stiffly from the waist to pick up the trowel and delivered it with both hands. Just as well he would never have to labour for a living – he would either rick his back or else his languid movements would lead to his dismissal. Since neither man acknowledged my arrival, I coughed.

'Earnest, I do hope you will introduce me?'

Discomfited at being caught performing menial work, my brother was brusque in his introduction.

'As you are already aware, Verger, this is Patience Leaton, my younger sister.'

'Younger by a matter of mere minutes,' I pointed out.

It was improper of me to qualify my brother's statement in front of our social inferior but Earnest let it pass. Verger proffered his filthy hand, and even though I shrank from him, the insolent man continued holding it out. No stranger to dealing with lowly folk, I flushed, strangely off-kilter. My heedless brother failed to ease the situation, leaving me no option but to shake Verger's hand by the fingertips.

'Twins, are you?' he asked, brow wrinkled in disbelief.

A reaction made more insulting for its being commonplace. My brother was sharp-boned, sharp-eyed and patrician like my father. With my downturned brows, eyes and mouth, my features appeared to be sliding from my face so I resembled a dog pleading for its life. Fortunately, nothing in my demeanour bore out this characteristic.

'Whose grave is that?' I demanded.

'It belongs to me mother, Rose Verger,' said the sexton. 'She died in childbed, so I never knew her.'

Verger's tragic start in life presented me with an opportunity, so I took it.

'How sad for you,' I said, with as much feeling as I could muster. 'Our mother died of that same malady, which is to be expected with twins.'

Earnest stiffened at my side but did not contradict me.

'My sister finished her off,' he added. 'Patience was born blue, strangled on her own cord, which explains a great deal about her behaviour to this very day.'

The part about being born blue was true, at least. The day of my birth had almost been the day of my death. My parents cared little whether I lived or died once they had their precious son. Were it not for the attending nun, Mother would have tossed me onto the fire, but despite surviving, I had suffered with a sickly constitution ever since.

'Sorry to hear that, lad. Still, you and your sister will be a great comfort to your father.'

'Indeed,' I replied. 'He used to call us Joy in Sorrow until we begged him to stop, and he has only recently reverted to calling us by our Christian names.'

My brother cleared his throat. 'But please, Verger, do not remind Father of it, for fear he resumes using the ghastly term instead of just plain Earnest and Patience.'

We were imprecisely named, the pair of us. My brother was equally apathetic whether it came to his studies or his religious duties, and I was as restive as a young hare in the majority of matters. My mother to blame again and further evidence of her lack of judgement.

'Divvent fash,' said the sexton. 'Your secret's safe with me...'

As Verger trailed off, he turned to the valley where a red-haired girl climbed steadily towards us, a collie to heel, and carrying a shepherd's crook in her left hand. Immodestly attired in an undyed wool frock, her matching cloak flowed behind her. About my age and perhaps half the age of the sexton. He raised a hand and received a wave of the crook and a wag of the tail in return.

'Who is that?' asked my brother, depriving me of the chance to remark upon her colouring.

'That fair maiden,' said the sexton, with something approaching reverence, 'is Rose.'

'So you like this wench?' enquired my brother in a tone of voice as stiff as his spine.

The sexton snorted. 'She's no wench, but I do think a lot of the lass.'

'She is very young for you.'

'Aye, she is, lad. Amongst other things.'

Both men were tense and I hoped they would not fight over a low woman. It would not be my brother's first lapse, but he promised me that he had mended his morals since the incident with our former housekeeper. He was forever apologising and labouring the point that he was a mere student back then, his head turned by a woman old enough to know better, but as it transpired, not old enough to be barren.

'You never mentioned her family name,' I said. 'Is Rose one of the Driver clan?'

The sexton nodded.

'Then call her over,' said my brother, 'so we can exchange a few words.'

'Little point in that. If the lass wants to grace us with her presence, she will, invitation or none. And if she's no fancy for it, no amount of asking will persuade her.'

Her obstinacy was no doubt born of being left-handed. Father would not permit it and forced his schoolboys to favour the right hand or suffer the consequences. Stubborn and sinistral, she may be, but my brother had taken a shine to the girl, although I doubted she would be interested in him with the big sexton present.

For a working man, Verger had a strong jaw and square shoulders, and his red hair and beard made him as vivid and handsome as a fox. Standing in the sexton's shadow, Earnest, with his floppy black hair and pale complexion, was merely a plain badger. Rose Driver appeared not to share this opinion. As she drew near, she shook her tumbling red locks over her shoulder, revealing her long, white throat.

Earnest was enchanted. Fortunately, Father was not here to witness this amoral display. With every day that passed, it became more apparent that Earnest suffered from the same affliction as Mother. Evidence that I needed to pray harder. No one spoke for some time until the sexton broke the silence.

'Hello, Rose. Miss Driver, I should say.'

'Hello, Mr Verger.'

'This here is Earnest Leaton.'

'Hello, Mr Leaton,' she replied, her dimpled smile showing remarkably straight teeth.

My brother held out his refined white hand and she seized it with her work-roughened paw, and it was hard to say which of them was the more surprised.

'An honour to meet you, Miss Driver.'

'And this is his twin sister, Patience Leaton,' said the sexton. 'Their father's the new minister. This is Rose Driver, from the farmstead down by the river.'

'Morning, Miss Leaton,' she said, smiling even wider. 'And this is Barebones.' On hearing its name, the collie bitch slunk forwards to lie at its owner's feet.

Perhaps hoping to ingratiate himself with its mistress, my brother stooped to rub the collie's ears. The creature growled and he stepped away, wrong-footed, and was only prevented from toppling by an ancient yew behind him. How unlike Earnest to be so awkward.

'Barebones?' I asked. 'That is a rather dangerous appellation. Is your bitch named for the preacher or the parliament of that name?'

She shrugged. 'Couldn't tell you. Reverend Foster named her. She was the ninth pup and he fetched her to me, tucked under his cloak. We couldn't get an ounce to stay on her. Hence the name.'

'Judging by the creature's sleek flanks,' I commented, 'she no longer suffers from that complaint.'

I ran my eyes up and down Rose Driver, for she was equally sleek, and her nervous laughter confirmed that my barb had found its target, but she did not drop her gaze and continued mopping and mowing at my brother. Thomas Verger busied himself with a piece of wood, his knobbly hand drawing the saw back and forth through a log. Despite the gelid weather, he was lightly clad in snug worsted breeches and a frayed cambric shirt, his moving flesh indecently visible beneath the threadbare garment. All the whilst, my brother and this girl were engaged in conversation, and it would have been improper had I not been present as chaperone. Although they were standing on hallowed ground in broad daylight and in full view of the church, there was no saying what could happen, especially given my brother's predilections. I scowled to show my displeasure at their frivolity but they were oblivious.

'Miss Driver, would you do me a favour?' asked the sexton and waited for the girl to tear her pretty green eyes away from my brother long enough to listen to his request.

'Aye, Mr Verger. What is it?'

'Could you fetch a few flowers from your Grandmother Chandler's garden? Some snowdrops for me mother's grave and some for your mam and little brother if you please? Mebbes some primroses and daffodils if the snow hasn't finished them afore they've started.'

She nodded and spoke most immodestly to Earnest, who was more than happy to accompany her.

'Wait for me,' I said, anxious not to leave them alone.

'Why not stay here with me, Miss Leaton, and tell me how your da likes everything done?'

Interrupted by the sexton, I missed my chance and Rose Driver and her new suitor vanished behind the manse, walking a little too close together for decency, their hips touching lightly as they swayed. Laughing and happy. Never had I seen my brother more closely resemble my mother, and it did my heart no good at all.

But perhaps I was being too hasty and this troubling situation might be turned to our advantage. The Leaton name had been tarnished in recent months, but no one in this parish knew our reputation and it might be worth investigating the Drivers' financial situation. A wealthy father-in-law could buy my brother a benefice and spare him the indignity of going to sea as a ship's chaplain. First though, Earnest would have to tie up Rose Driver's left hand until she stopped favouring it, and Father would have to forgive her family's outstanding fines.

The Cade Lamb

ROSE

At dawn, I nudged Barebones awake and dragged a fleece over my shoulders. Even the thought of leaving the shepherd's hut and going outside into the drifts filled me with dread, but there was no choice. My flock was ready to yean, regardless of the weather, and they wouldn't all survive in these low temperatures. The muffled silence outside was a sure sign that more snow had fallen. Last night, I'd returned to the hut, worn out, cold and wet, with my cloak and kirtle encrusted, despite hitching them above my knee. They'd hung overnight but the hems remained damp, though it hardly mattered as they'd soon be soaked again.

The hardest part of the day, this, bracing myself to go out to work, even though the thought of it was always worse than the experience. It was beyond me why such tender creatures entered the world in the cruellest month – swapping a hot belly for a howling snowstorm. We bred them to be born in spring when nourishing grass abounded, but April was ever the knave. Some years, the lambing season started with sunshine and flowers pushing through the earth, only for the sky to whiten again. It made for hardy young, I supposed. If the frail souls could survive such brutal hill weather, they should survive almost anything.

From my crocks, I cut two thick slices each of salted porridge and potted beef into our bowls and placed one on the floor for the ravenous collie. Judging by the bitter weather, she'd be eating more than beef porridge come nightfall. Nourished, if not warm, I pulled on my kirtle and boots, wrapped a muffler round my neck, drew on my cloak and tied it with a belt hung with the tools needed for the day. Last, I put on fingerless sheepskin mittens to protect my hands while still allowing me to work. When I pushed open the door into the half-light, the icy wind whipped my breath away, so I pushed my muffler up over my mouth and nose. On a clear day, I could see the mountains and hills of Scotland, but today the sky was no more than a smudge of grey behind the blizzard. I stepped down into the snow, cringing as it reached above my boots, chilling my calves and knees through my woollen stockings.

We crept under the shelter of some nearby crags to relieve ourselves, then my next job was to dig out the fodder shed. The biggest problem was holding the gravid ewes back. It wasn't beyond them to batter down the door and Da had repaired the hinges twice already this year. Barebones more than earned her keep by holding the flock at bay while I cleared away a bale's width of snow to get me into the shed. If it wasn't for the collie running rings around them, the hungry horde would be inside with me. Always famished in the final week or two before lambing, and more so in these freezing conditions. Backside first, I pushed my way out of the shed, hauling a bale of hay-grass, and dropped the latch behind me. My fingers were clumsy and it was a tussle to unfasten the binding rope and get the hay into the feeders before the ewes flattened me, Barebones or each other.

I kept close watch on them while they ate. Most of them were heavier than me and if they ended up cast, it was a task getting them on their feet again. While they were busy eating, I counted them, using my crook to mark five-bar gates in the snow. Twenty-three. Two were missing. No sheep would ever willingly miss a meal at the best of times, let alone while heavily pregnant and in a storm, and they hated being alone. Not being with their sisters meant they must be dead, stuck or in lamb. Hopefully, the latter.

'Seek, Barebones. Seek.'

The dog pricked up her ears, turned into the wind and scented the air.

'Go on, lass,' I said, bending into the blizzard and following her until the air carried a faint bleat to me. It was exhausting, pressing forwards through the drifts, face wet and stinging, chest burning with the effort and my feet already numb. The driving snow blinded me but I dragged myself towards the sound of my lost sheep. The crook helped keep me upright, but between the white sky and the white hills, the constant flurrying made it hard to tell which way was up and it would be all too easy to tumble over the edge of a high ridge.

A distant hump told me the ewe was in trouble. With luck, she was stranded and would only need digging out. She'd sheltered under a crag, but the wind cutting across the tops had covered her in snow. I unhooked the small shovel from my belt, wondering – not for the first time – why I'd chosen the hardest of jobs. The cattle were snug in the barn, where their young would birth safely, close to the farmhouse. But I loved my dear sheep – their woolliness, their peacefulness, their hardiness – I just didn't like the weather on these hills.

The runaway ewe hadn't been hardy enough. A seasoned lamber, she'd ruptured and bled to death by the looks of her. Her ram lamb was also dead, but by some miracle, his sister gave a piteous bleat. Snug between two still-warm corpses, she'd been sheltered from the worst of the storm. Gently, I tucked the survivor into my chemise, tightened my bodice and covered her with my cloak. The return journey was less fraught with the wind to my back and the blizzard easing off as I walked. The orphan reached the hut alive, and if one of the other ewes birthed a singleton lamb today, she might be persuaded to adopt this little cade and feed it alongside her own.

Once the newborn was cosy in a fleece-lined box, I left her. The end of the blizzard had tempted the birds out and I noticed a dozen or so ravens cawing and swooping above a small hollow – the other missing ewe. Barebones raced forwards, scattering them. I followed, breathless, knowing that the ravens had beaten me to it. The labouring ewe bleated in misery but it hadn't stopped the ravens from gouging out her lamb's eyes and tongue with their cruel beaks. Poor soul wasn't yet fully birthed and its life was over. Barebones pranced and barked at them while I murmured to the mother, trying my best to calm her.

'Not long, lass. Not long, and you shall have your bairn.'

It was the worst thing I ever had to do in my shepherding but it had to be done and fast. I delivered the corpse, tucked it into my bodice and hurried to yon side of the shepherd's hut where I'd be out of sight of the bereft ewe. I turned my back to the flock, who were browsing the hay. While they were occupied, I began the grim task of flenching, but as I pierced the skin of the dead lamb, my hand slipped and I cut myself, which did not ease my work. Despite my bloody hand and numb fingers, I managed to cut around the lamb's throat to free up its shoulders. I nicked it left and right and tied its forelegs to the wheel of my hut. There, I pulled firmly on the skin, peeling it back to reveal the delicate form beneath. Finally, I wedged the skinned carcass back into my bodice and my knife into my belt before entering the hut with the tailed hide.

Inside the hut, the lonesome cade bleated. Quickly, I swaddled the orphan in the makeshift jerkin. From outside, Barebones growled and the lamb quivered. It wasn't like her to give warning when there wasn't a soul in sight, so I silenced the dog and ordered her into the hut. She did as told and slunk inside. The cade continued to tremble as I carried it to the grieving ewe and nudged it close to its new mother. Shivering more from the awful deed than from the cold, I waited and watched until the ewe snuffled at her dead lamb's tail – a sure sign of acceptance. Backing away, I reversed into someone and jumped, causing the flenching knife to fall from my belt. I turned to face my assailant and there stood the new vicar's daughter, black hair plastered to her snow-scalded face. Neither her clothes nor her constitution were fit for these conditions.

'What are you doing out here in this weather?' I asked. 'You'll catch your death if you're not careful.'

Although open-mouthed, she never said a word. As I bent to retrieve my knife, my cloak opened, revealing the skinned corpse poking out of my bodice. The girl wailed, an awful keening sound that would frighten the flock, who were already under duress, so I put a hand out to shush her. When the girl saw the knife in my blood-soaked hand, her eyes bulged. She knocked the blade from me, turned and ran screaming down the hill towards the river, skidding and slipping in the snow as she went. At the valley bottom, she skated over the frozen river, almost setting her neck, but righted herself and started the difficult ascent to the church. What on earth had fetched her out in such terrible weather? I'd half a mind to go after the ignorant girl and explain what she'd seen – perhaps she was from a city and not familiar with animal husbandry – but decided against it. I had no time for chasing after the silly miss when I had so much to see to, and Patience Leaton would soon learn our customs.

An Unholy Experience

PATIENCE

As if the hellish sight of Rose Driver's blood sacrifice were not enough, her death threat filled me with dread. I ran away to seek sanctuary, but my poor town shoes were no match for the ice, and every step forwards cost me two backwards. Crossing the frozen river was treacherous, although it held my slight weight and I made my way up the slick bank by clawing at the thorny undergrowth, scratching my hands in my haste. It was as if nature had awoken at the behest of the shepherdess, intent on preventing my escape, and the driving snow combined with my tears to blind me to the path ahead.

I could not see Rose Driver behind me, but she had no need to follow me in person with the whole of nature at her command. Terrified for my soul, I kept climbing. It was a hellish ascent, with some evil force dragging me back until I reached the lych gate, that blessed entrance to hallowed ground. The proximity of the church lent strength to my shaking legs and I skidded onwards through the narthex, finally pressing my palms to the church door. My heart slowed instantly, but being on the threshold would not save me, so I heaved open the door and stumbled into the nave. I crossed the chancel and prostrated myself at the foot of the altar, begging the Lord for His blessing. My heart fluttered against the cold stone, and when sunlight streamed through the lancets, warming the sacred space, I wept with joy at being saved, sending up prayers of thanks.

Hours passed before Earnest found me. He wrapped my shivering form in his cloak and wiped my face. The calming presence of my brother allowed me to relay to him, between sobs and gasps, the horror of what had passed. My original aim had been to visit the Drivers' farmstead to secure a promise to amend their behaviour and present themselves at the next Sunday service. However, on my way there, I noticed the shepherdess on the opposite hill, so I changed course. What better symbol of Christ than someone tending her flock? My idea was to revert at least one Driver to the fold, with an eye to assessing her suitability for marriage to Earnest.

What I had initially perceived as a pleasing pastoral scene, symbolic of the Almighty, turned out to be more worthy of Satan. As I drew near, I witnessed Rose Driver in the monstrous act of skinning a defenceless lamb and dressing another in its bloodstained fleece. The woman had sliced open her hand, allowing her blood to commingle with that of the dead lamb to seal her satanic pact.

So bewildering was the sight that all my senses escaped me, leaving me mute. I had surprised the hag in some gruesome rite, yet she carried on, unaware of my presence. The shock prevented me from moving or speaking until she reversed into me. Red of hair. Green of eye. Bloody of hand. With a skinned corpse crushed against her heart. No shepherdess this, but witch!

The hag wasted no time and snatched up her knife, no doubt hellbent on skinning me as well, and the devil only knew what she would clothe in my skin. Merciful God granted me strength to knock the knife from her hand and I fled the way I had come, threats of death ringing in my ears.

I sought the sanctuary of the church, knowing that a true witch could never enter a consecrated building.

Earnest listened to my account without interruption. When I was spent and sat panting against him, he picked me up. Wordless, he carried me to the manse, and up the stairs to my chamber, where he deposited me on my bed.

'Get some sleep, sister. There will be a rational explanation. Do not speak to Father of witches, else it rakes up old memories. And do not cause trouble for Rose Driver. I am warning you, Patience. For now, I must leave but will return to light a fire.'

With that, my brother left, concerned not a jot for my health – corporeal or spiritual – saving his sympathy for the latest apple of his eye. Well, she could not be his wife now, not after seeing what I had seen, and not now that I knew her to be a consort of the devil.

🖤

When I awoke, the room was dark and cold. So much for Earnest lighting a fire. Father sat in a chair beside me, wrapped in a blanket, head bowed in prayer. When I spoke, he raised his head and blinked. Despite my unholy experience, I summoned the strength to explain what had happened, but that considerate man would not permit me to exert myself further.

'Do not trouble yourself, dear child. Your brother relayed the grisly tale to me and my constitution will not stand a second telling.' He placed his dry hand on my clammy forehead and closed his eyes. 'You are quite safe, Patience, but refrain from adventuring in the low quarters of the parish. Do no more than sleep and eat until you are in your right temper.'

'But the Drivers...' I struggled to sit up. 'Their non-observance puts them in spiritual danger. I planned to interrogate them and fetch them home to Christ, but this...

this witch waylaid me. And make no mistake, Father, for that is what she is. We must do something about her. She is a fiend.'

'My dear girl, you are feverish. Let us hear no more of the Drivers, or of witches or fiends. Conserve your strength.' He rubbed vigorously at the furrows that had appeared on his forehead. 'Rest and revive. Do not dwell further on what you saw this morning. I fear there has been some misinterpretation on your part. What you witnessed this morning is likely some rural ritual with a plausible explanation, but do not worry yourself further about such matters. In the morning, your brother will investigate in your stead and once he has reported to me, I will determine what action to take, if any. In the meantime, I will fetch you a bowl of clear broth.'

'O, but I cannot eat before I have been blessed and until then, I should fast.'

Father inhaled and exhaled heavily through his nose and made the sign of the cross over me.

'I have blessed you, Patience, and that is enough. No more fasting. We have discussed this at length in the past. Broth, and perhaps no more praying for the present. Broth and rest, and that is all. I forbid you to brood on this incident. Do you hear me?'

I nodded but neither he nor Earnest could compel me to eat against my will, and nobody but the Lord could prevent me from praying.

⁂

My prayers, however, were interrupted by some uninvited visitors, each carrying a small sack. Two women stood at the scullery step, barely dressed for the harsh conditions, making it only too apparent how pleasingly each woman filled her vestments. The younger woman looked to be four or five years older than me and the elder perhaps a decade or two her senior. Each had eyes the colour of forget-me-knots and hair of gold. The elder was married and her hair was decently covered, although stray tendrils had escaped at her temples, whilst the other woman's hair was brazenly uncovered. Mother and daughter perhaps, although the age gap did not seem large enough, so I judged them to be sisters. By the looks of their pink complexions and heaving chests, they had recently climbed the steep hill from the valley.

'Are you the vicar's lass?' enquired the married woman in the thick, local dialect.

'Whilst I would not put it in quite those terms, I am Patience Leaton, yes. What brings you?'

'I hoped to discuss some family matters and also to ask about some work for my sister in exchange for bed and board. Might I speak to your father?'

My first instinct was to turn them away until it struck me that I had not seen them in church yesterday. No one could forget such startling looks. They must be part of the Driver clan. On closer questioning, it emerged that the elder woman was May Driver, married to Farmer Driver. Her unmarried sister, Matilda Green, lived with them. Whilst clearly of proletarian stock, both women were unusually beautiful, Matilda slightly more so, and possibly why Goodwife Driver wanted her gone. Her husband must have a roving eye and the older sister risked being put out to pasture. It would be diverting to hire Matilda Green, who might shed some light on the Drivers' absenteeism. On top of which, I had not the slightest desire to spend my days drudging in the upkeep of the manse.

'Wait there,' I said and shut the door.

Father, labouring over his sermon, expressed more than a little dismay at my interruption.

'Goodwife Driver and Spinster Green have presented themselves, seeking an audience. The goodwife wishes to discuss matters familial whilst the spinster wishes to apply for a live-in post with us. She currently resides with the Drivers...'

I raised my brows to indicate my ulterior motive but my parent was in no mood for intrigue and set down his pen rather more smartly than was strictly necessary.

'What post, Patience? We have no such thing, live-in or otherwise. My stipend is scarcely ample for the three of us, never mind a fourth. Send them on their way.'

'You cannot possibly expect me to keep house, and it occurred to me, Father, that if you fine the Drivers properly, it would more than pay for Spinster Green's services. Besides, if my mother were still here, you would need to feed and clothe her, so I fail to see the difference.'

At the mention of Mother, my father's face closed. I had overstepped by mentioning her. It always put him out of temper, albeit momentarily, but I was nothing if not resolute so tried again.

'Spinster Green is lowly but has excellent carriage and a fine complexion. I had no opportunity to inspect her teeth closely but at first glance they appeared sound. In addition to which, you may be saving an innocent soul. If the Drivers cannot or will not attend church, you should rescue the girl from that godless family.'

He sighed. 'Fetch them in. You know I can never resist saving a lost soul.'

When I opened the door again, neither woman had slouched in my absence, nor were they picking their teeth, as so many underlings often did once out of sight of their betters.

'Father will hear you. Quick sharp, the pair of you.'

The women stepped inside, admiring the interior of our home. I led them to my father's writing corner, where they stood with heads lowered, suitably humble.

Father brightened considerably when he saw his visitors, and I knew he would stretch his stipend to take them both on, should the opportunity arise. He stood up and beckoned them to sit at our table.

'Good evening, Goodwife Driver and Spinster Green. I take it you are two of the parish's most steadfast sinners?'

Goodwife Driver smiled prettily and proceeded to fob off her parish priest with promises of church attendance once the lambing ended.

'It's a busy life, farming, and never more so than when the lambing starts.' She fossicked in her sack, drawing out a smoked leg of mutton. 'A gesture of goodwill from my family to yours.'

Her shrewdness astonished me. This welcome gift was a thinly disguised bribe and delivered by a messenger so fetching that it was all but impossible for my father to insist on fines, even though a few mutton suppers would barely put a dent in the monies owed. No wonder his predecessor had given in to the Drivers so easily and so often if they bought him off in this fashion.

'Agreed, Goodwife Driver, you may get the lambing season out of the way.' My gullible parent smiled and wagged a finger. 'But once the dale is littered by ewes with lambs at foot, we will expect you at every Sunday service.'

Listen to my father, sounding every inch the country farmer! Goodwife Driver dropped her gaze by way of reply and surely I could not be alone in noticing that she had neatly avoided making any formal pledge to abide by this agreement.

'As to the employment of your sister...' Father turned to the younger woman. 'Would you like to help us here at the manse, my dear?'

Spinster Green nodded furiously. Keenness was a worthy quality in a servant and this one would be very easy to bend to my will.

'Pray, stop wringing your hands and show them to me.'

Obediently, she held them out and turned them over for inspection when my father tapped them. Chapped and calloused, but clean, with the nails neatly trimmed and not chewed.

'All members of my household must attend church twice a day in the week and thrice on Sundays and high holy days. Is that agreeable to you?'

The girl nodded. 'Aye, that it is, sir.'

Her sister was busy looking through the window at the dark hills to the west during this transaction. My father should have made Green's employment conditional upon the Drivers attending church, but his mind was addled by our present company.

'Good,' said my father. 'Then start at once. There is a garret where you may sleep.'

Whilst most men were beasts, Father was a godly man, who never failed to overcome the devil's temptation, but my brother was an entirely different kettle of fish.

'O, Father, you cannot let a servant sleep in the attic. She can bed down with me.' That should prevent any mischief arising.

'Come, Patience, I hardly think that would be acceptable to Spinster Green.'

As if she should have any say in the matter, but she did not demur.

'Aye, Minister Leaton. That'll be grand. At the minute, I share with Rosie Driver and she's so lanky, she takes up more than half–'

'Even so,' said Father, cutting off the talkative girl. 'We are not short of chambers here, so you will have your own. Not another word, Patience.'

Father ran quickly through her expected duties. Our new servant would rise before the family each morning to light the fires, and she would lie down last thing at night after locking up and snuffing the candles. My father did not want to see or hear Green whilst she toiled. The girl would have to become like a shadow, fathoming out where he might be at any given hour of the day and avoiding that place. In exchange for her labour, she would receive bed and board and a shilling a week, to be paid in arrears on each quarter day. She might expect no gratuities as the Leatons did not hold with tipping servants for doing what they had already been paid to do. And she would be given a Sunday afternoon off once per month.

'If those terms are agreeable, you may fetch your belongings – if you have any – and commence forthwith.'

'I have this sack and what I stand up in, Minister Leaton, sir. So I can start straight away.'

'Then start you shall. We eat sparely, but we like to eat on time, four times a day. I take my food plain, as God intended, with a meagre serving of salt for the sake of health. My daughter will equip you with the details. Stand up and turn around for me.'

Ever amenable, she rotated, and he ran his eyes all over her, frowning.

'The wool of your frock is admirably undyed, Spinster Green, but it is too close-fitting and cut very low, which may prove distracting to my son, who is still of an impressionable age. Patience, outfit the girl in something plain of yours, and when she is appropriately attired and set to work, return to me.'

❦

I picked out last year's frock, which had a sufficiently modest neckline. The indigo drained our servant's colouring to the point of drabness. Unfortunately, whilst Green was about my height, she filled out my frock so much that I was afraid for the seams. Father did right to be concerned about distracting my brother. Matilda Green would distract the most decent man, and Earnest was far from being that. Although Green was unmarried, with no need to cover her golden locks, I thought to balance the scales in Earnest's favour. Once fastened into an apron and coif, she was quite homely, and the straining seams would be resolved in time by reduced rations. After instructing Green on our habits and preferences, I left her preparing our supper and returned to my father.

'Now that we have spared the soul of one member of the Driver household, Father, it remains to be seen what can be done for the rest of that troubled family, and I must begin with the witch, so I will just–'

'You will just nothing, Patience. Your brother will visit Miss Driver at first light. I have asked him to investigate what went on between you and the shepherdess. Until we hear back from him, we will have no more mention of witches. Do I make myself clear?'

'Yes, Father. Very clear.'

Somewhat unnecessarily, he then scolded me about keeping out of mischief, explaining that as Green would take responsibility for all the workings of the house, the devil would create work for my idle hands, and he counselled me to find myself a new diversion. He went so far as to list what he considered suitable occupations for young ladies. I assured him that supervising the help would be sufficiently time-consuming. If Father thought I had time to waste on visiting the sick and the poor of the parish, he was sadly mistaken. I had God's work to attend to, and Matilda Green, whilst so far ignorant of my plans, would help me to achieve my ends.

Hailstorm

ROSE

The moaning wind and creaking timbers woke me, but Barebones was already on full alert. So far, the ancient shepherd's hut had never been known to tilt, but the wind was overdue its chance. Da had caulked the timbers, but not too tightly, for fear we sail across the Pennines and into a neighbouring dale. Through tiny cracks, warm air and light streamed in, brushing my cheek. The wind carried the promise of a thaw, which raised my spirits, but it was no good lying abed wondering about the weather when it was time to get up and go to work. I hoped the orphan had survived the night. While we broke our fast, I slid back the hatch to check the weather. The dale was still snow-covered, but the sun had washed the hill yon side of the river in a watery gold so the manse and the church shone. Halfway down that hill, a man struggled to keep his feet. No more than a small crow in his dark clothes against the immense expanse of silver sky and white hills. At this distance, I couldn't tell whether it was Minister Leaton or his son, but whoever it was, he'd likely come bearing a complaint. Not much else would draw a body out in this weather. I stroked Barebones to still the growl rumbling in her throat.

He ran downhill the last few hundred yards, slipping and

sliding towards the river. The air was much warmer today than yesterday and already softening the snow. The river wasn't safe to cross, but he managed to pick his way over without breaking the ice and clambered uphill. Someone really should tell the Leatons about the ford before one of them went through the ice and drowned. When he drew nearer, I saw his hair was black and not silver, so it was the son and not the father. I waited until Earnest Leaton was within ten yards, then opened the door and stood back to let him inside. His boots and breeches were soaked and he sat down, shivering. I threw him my sheepskin, which he pulled around his shoulders, and I noticed for the first time how long and elegant his fingers were. I'd never seen such hands. He must have felt my curious stare for he soon curled them beneath the fleece.

My visitor was a lot taller than his sister, though they both looked equally underfed. That would change since Tilly had gone to keep for the Leatons, and she'd take delight in feeding them up. Da was furious that she'd left us, and of course May had borne the brunt of his temper. Part of me wondered how much of Da's fury really had to do with losing a good cook, let alone one so comely. May was wise, finding her younger sister a safe haven before my father took his urgency for a son elsewhere. I liked this boy. Man, I supposed. For twins, the Leatons weren't alike, apart from their build and colouring. Unlike his sister, Earnest was beautiful. Slender and pale, his cheekbones looked in danger of breaking the skin. His grey eyes were so light they were almost silver, and he had a cleft chin. Dimple in chin, devil within – if the mart wives were to be believed. Oddly, I found myself unable to meet his gaze and looked at my feet. It wasn't like me to be bashful – an honest dales lass who'd been raised to look everyone square in the eye.

'If this is April,' he said, breaking the silence, 'then I am afraid for December.'

'You'll sharp get used to the weather. It's not too bad in

the dale. You just never know what to expect on the tops. But June, July and August are often reliably free of ice.'

'As many as three months?'

I nodded and tried not to smile too readily because I could guess at the reason for his visit. 'Your sister sent you?'

'My father sent me but on account of Patience and your most recent meeting.'

'I see.' The word *meeting* hardly began to describe yesterday's events. After she'd knocked the knife from my hand, the stricken girl had hared off without giving me a chance to explain.

'My sister has made herself quite ill.'

'I'm sure she has, but the ewes are in lamb and they wait for no man, even the son of a minister, so this discussion will have to wait.'

His knitted brows and pursed lips told me that Earnest Leaton was not a young man used to waiting.

'Then I will accompany you, and we can talk while you work.'

'No, you won't. You're a stranger so you'll disquiet my flock, and they're doubly agitated by pregnancy and the temperature as it is. You can stop here till you dry out a bit and then go home. I'll come and find you once the lambing season's over.' With that, I pulled on my cloak and boots. 'When I've gone, strip off those wet clothes, but be warned, it's not much warmer in here than it is out there.'

He pulled a long face and raised a booted foot. 'Since my fingers are still numb with cold, perhaps you might oblige me?'

I'd grown up watching Granny and May taking Granda and Da's boots off. Two full-grown men, each more than capable of removing their own boots, and May and Granny with more than enough work to be getting on with.

'Rub your hands together till the feeling comes back to your fingers and you'll be able to see to yourself.'

'So, you're going to leave me alone after I half-killed myself to come and see you?'

'My sole reason for being up here is to tend my flock and nobody asked you to come.' I fastened my belt and picked up my crook. 'Get yourself home once you're dry and keep off the river unless you're sick of living. That ice won't last the day. Follow the river south till you reach the ford – it's not far. And don't stay here too long. If you're found in my hut, it'll ruin me and do you no favours either.'

'Have no fear. I will be gone by sunset. Father would be disappointed if he caught me unchaperoned at night with a woman.'

This was just about the most remote place in the whole of England in the summer and more so in conditions like these, but it wasn't unheard of for Da to come up with fresh rations. Minister Leaton might be disappointed with his son for keeping my company but there would be blood spilt if Da got wind of a man in here, minister's son or not.

Cold weather always made it hard to drag myself outside, but today I had an added temptation – one that was pleasing to the eye and whose company wasn't terrible. But with my belly filled, I had no excuse for tarrying. I clicked my tongue and Barebones followed me out.

Once we'd relieved ourselves, we walked to the feed shed. The ewes huddled together, trying to stand clear of the rapidly melting snow and the resulting clarts. As soon as they saw me, the sheep started running for the feed shed.

'Come by, Barebones, come by.'

Before the woolly mass could jostle around the shed and make it impossible for me to get in, the dog circled them long enough for me to prise the door open and drag a bale to the feeders. The famished flock wasted no time once the dog released them and charged forwards to break their fast, leaving the cade lamb shivering and alone before she scrambled to catch up with her new mother. The lamb was scrawny but alive, with her little overcoat and tail still intact, and the mother hadn't rejected her so far.

While the flock ate, I counted them. No more lambs yet, but I was missing a ewe. Barebones sniffed the air and loped off. I tailed her to a steep rise where the missing ewe was struggling to give birth. Poor lass was tired from her labours, but the forelegs and head were showing, so I eased out the lamb and left the mother to lick her newborn. They were both doing well, so I kept my distance and watched over them in case of predators. When the ewe was recovered and the lamb suckled and thriving, Barebones drove them back to the flock. I spent the rest of the day separating and examining the other ewes. Most of their udders were starting to firm up, but none of their vulvas were ripe.

Over the last hour or so, the sky had turned from silver to pewter even though nightfall was a way off. Above me, dense clouds loured over the moors. After the promising start to the day, this bleak sky troubled me. It wasn't like anything I'd ever seen before.

The ewes knew something was coming and they'd crammed themselves beneath an overhang at the foot of a high ridge. The newborn was feeding well and the cade's mother was still suckling her. None of the other ewes showed any signs of going into labour, and they were sheltered, so I set off to the hut with a clear conscience, dog padding beside me. We ploughed uphill through clarts and streaming water, and as we neared the hut the door opened, revealing Earnest.

'Get inside,' I shouted. 'Before someone sees you.'

His complexion darkened but he did as told. Outside, I kicked the steps to shake off the clarts and brushed down Barebones. Once I had the thick of it cleared off me and the dog, I opened the door and followed her inside.

He smiled at me. 'Instead of braving the elements twice, I decided to wait for your return. Once you are dry, perhaps we could quickly discuss my sister and the need for you and your family to return to church before the month-end. Then I will leave you to your meal and your bed.'

I struggled to hold my temper after he'd ignored my instruction, but he was here now, I supposed, and another hour could do no harm. Night hadn't yet fallen and he had been sent by the vicar.

'After we've *all* eaten, we can discuss whatever you like, and when that's done, feel free to leave. As for going to church, that's something to take up with Da. He won't let any of us across the threshold.' He opened his mouth to speak but I continued. 'It's no good asking me why, because I'm no wiser than you are when it comes to my da's reasoning.'

This was a barefaced lie on my part. We didn't go to church because of my reaction to going to church one Easter Sunday when I was very small, but I wasn't going to tell Earnest Leaton that.

He frowned. 'Very well, I will speak to your father immediately an opportunity presents itself.'

It would serve my guest right to eat some of our fare. I sliced a portion each of porridge and beef into Barebones' bowl and set it down for her.

'You feed the dog first?'

'Rightly so,' I said. 'She's worked hard all day.' I cut another portion of porridge and beef into my bowl and handed it to him. I'd eat my share straight from the crock. 'There's only the one spoon, so you'll have to wait your turn.'

He put a hand to his belt and untied a silver spoon and eating knife.

'Always prepared for any eventuality.'

The silver spoon belonged at the manse and it irked me that some precious thing my mother and grandmother had once polished now belonged to this undeserving family. Reverend Foster had cared for every item in his charge, and here was one of his good spoons carelessly tied to the belt of Earnest Leaton where it could easily have been lost in the snow.

'Give me my sheepskin and turn away.' I stripped off my boots and outer clothes, hung them to dry and wrapped myself in the fleece. Having licked her bowl clean already, Barebones curled up and began to snore. Dry at last, I could eat my meal.

'Shall I say grace?'

I paused, spoon halfway to my mouth. 'Please yourself.'

He closed his eyes and lowered his head, while I watched his red lips murmuring the unfamiliar words.

'So,' he said, opening his eyes, 'about Patience.'

'When I'm finished eating.'

'Peace,' he said, and we ate in silence.

Did Earnest always eat so slowly, or was he being polite on my account? I wasn't used to slow eating or good manners. He smiled at me and put down his spoon, half his meal uneaten.

'No, keep going,' I said. 'Take your time. I'm not used to seeing a man still eating after I've finished. At home, Da eats his dinner as if someone were about to take it from him.'

'And so he should. An honest farmer eating an honest meal after his day at labour. When I leave here, I'll walk to the farmhouse and speak to your father about the family's failure to observe the sabbath. On my way back, I'll fetch you some more rations. I'm sorry to leave you short.'

'And so you should be.' I tried to imagine Earnest challenging Da and feared for his safety. 'Listen, there's a bad sky out there and it's setting in dark long before time. We've not been to church in a few years, so a few more days won't matter. And as for supplies, divvent fash, Da is bound to come by. So get yourself away home.'

'You might have a point. But so my day isn't entirely wasted, if we could just quickly discuss my sister. Yesterday,

I found her prone at the foot of the altar. She takes everything to heart, you see, and she's quite unwell.'

He covered his mouth with his hand and I saw how awkward it made him, revealing his sister's flaws.

'I've no idea what your sister thought she saw. She surprised me, that's all, and got hold of the wrong end of the stick.'

'It would not be the first time and she can get quite carried away. Why not tell me what actually happened?'

I explained it was usual practice with an orphan to clothe it in the skin of a dead lamb. Most often, the bereaved mother would pick up the scent of her own lamb and in her joy, ignore the scent of the cade beneath the fleece.

'It is quite a macabre act,' he said, 'if you don't mind my saying so.'

'It's not my favourite task, but the lamb gets a mother and the mother gets a lamb. Otherwise, the pair of them would pine to death, leaving me with two dead sheep.'

'But skinning a dead lamb.' He shuddered. 'Not the right kind of work for a beau... for a young woman like yourself.'

He blushed and I wondered whether he'd been about to say beautiful. How ridiculous. What would someone so learned and refined want with someone like me? But he did look at me closely till I had to drop my gaze.

'So,' I said, 'now we've cleared up that misunderstanding, you can go home.'

'Oh, of course. Yes.' He held up his bowl.

'Set it on the floor if you've finished.' I slid back the door hatch. 'Night's falling, so you really can't be here.'

'I wasn't thinking.' He smiled ruefully. 'Again.' He stood up and cleared his throat. 'Then, I will bid you goodnight, Rose. Might I have permission to darken your door again?'

Hearing this, my heart skipped but it wouldn't pay to appear too eager.

'You might, but don't darken this door, or Da will gut you.'

He grimaced at this, but seemed otherwise unafraid, so I told him to call on me at the farmhouse once the lambing was over and done with.

'When each ewe has a lamb or two at foot, it'll be safe to come calling. But you'd best be quick because the calving begins straight after.'

'Understood. And please accept my apology if I have compromised you. It was not my intent.'

Just as he reached for his cloak, there was a loud crack of thunder. Something hard hit the roof and I wondered about a lightning strike. The dog growled and her hackles went up, but when the crack was quickly followed by a fierce cannonade, Barebones ignored the racket and fell asleep.

I smiled at his bewilderment. 'Hail.'

'In April?'

'The weather takes no notice of the calendar in these parts, but it does sound heavy.' The hail showed no sign of stopping and I was glad the sheep were under shelter. Earnest got up to move to the door but I stuck out a leg to stop him.

'It sounds as though rocks are being dropped from heaven. I was going to put my head out to see what is going on.'

'And would you put your head out if rocks *were* falling from the sky?'

'Ah, no. Perhaps not.'

'Falling ice will split your head open just as easily as stone. I can't put you out in that and have your death on my conscience.'

I slid the hatch open an inch and peered out. All around, hailstones the size of cherries were piling up. It would take only one to concuss him, or worse. The hut was made from spliced saplings so its roof should withstand the hail, and it had to be safer staying under cover than going outside. When I turned, my uninvited guest was standing very close to me.

'You'll have to wait it out,' I said.

'How long might that take?' he asked, peering into my eyes.

'Hard to say,' I croaked. 'Never seen hail this size till the day.'

'I had better stay then, but what about your reputation?' he asked, winding a finger into my hair and tucking a tendril behind my ear.

'My reputation would be ruined and me with it.'

All he'd done was touch my hair, but my whole being sensed it and I stepped back as if stung. He took a step forwards. His breath was warm on my face, and my own breath came far too fast.

'Better to be alive and ruined,' he said, 'than dead and pious.'

The second the words were out of his mouth, his lips brushed mine and all thoughts of scandal were immediately forgotten.

A Dark Hand Moves Against Us

PATIENCE

After a hearty dinner of mutton stew and dumplings, I left the new servant preparing our next meal and retired to the refuge of my chamber for an afternoon nap. Green had a deft touch in the kitchen, but laboured under the impression that she was still feeding a barnful of farmers. Whilst Father expended a significant amount of energy during the delivery of his sermons, and in the crafting of them, my brother and I were more sedentary in our pursuits and needed less nourishment. Really, I should have gone out for a walk to aid my digestion but Father cautioned me about leaving the house again so soon.

The fire roared, giving off an intolerable heat. Exhausted by my brush with evil, I prayed for strength and collapsed onto my pillows. Sleep eluded me, however, so I examined the corniced ceiling, which always tired my eyes with its intricate patterns. What a waste of time, money and materials, especially upstairs where nobody but the occupant of the bed would notice it. It amazed me that a working man had wasted his hours on such frivolous labour.

Unable to sleep, I spent the remainder of the afternoon updating my journal to ensure a faithful record of my recent experience. Earnest had yet to reappear from his investigation of Rose Driver, so I would speak to him at supper and then amend my entry, depending on what he reported. I would also ask him about his failure to calculate the Drivers' outstanding fines. Granted, they had failed to observe the sabbath for some twenty years, and my brother preferred letters to numbers, but that should not have prevented him from working out what they owed. Some notional figure would suffice to frighten them into obedience. At this rate, Earnest would be off to sea and the Drivers would remain untouched. Thus far, not a single Leaton had set foot in their farmstead.

Humours restored, I arose and went downstairs to find Father at the dining table, holding a silver knife and fork. He had to use this cutlery, of course, as there was no simpler alternative available.

'Patience. I trust you are recovered and will eat some supper?'

On his porcelain plate were generous slices of smoked mutton and a hunk of bread. Goodwife Driver's gift. He savoured it, relishing the mutton as if feasting on the flesh of the woman herself. The pink meat immediately put me in mind of the skinned lamb I had seen.

'Perhaps just a drop of clear broth for me, Father.'

I shook his brass handbell to summon our servant.

'Yes, Minister Leaton,' said Green, slightly out of breath. 'What can I bring you?'

'No more for me, thank you, Spinster Green, but you may fetch my daughter some broth and some bread.'

Before I could object to the bread, Green addressed me.

'Are you any better, madam?'

Little did she know, but I would never be better. It was not her fault though, as someone with her rude health could never comprehend what it was like to suffer as I did, but I would not be unkind when she meant well, so I inclined my head slightly.

'Very good, madam,' she said and scampered back to the kitchen. When would the girl's enthusiasm wane?

Father chewed each mouthful twelve times to prevent overeating. Gluttons wolfed their food, whereas the truly devout savoured every morsel and thanked God for his bounty.

Whilst she set down my bowl, Father continued working through his pile of meat, and our inexperienced servant hovered uncertainly. She would need to learn when to be present and when to make herself scarce.

'Go and have your own dinner, Spinster Green,' said Father. 'My daughter and I will clear up after ourselves.'

She actually curtsied prior to departing, a gesture wasted on my father, who had eyes only for his supper.

Apart from saying grace, we did not speak again whilst eating, because Father frowned on anything that might disturb his digestion. The broth was so perfectly clarified that the gold leaf on the bottom of my plate was visible. My unholy experience had weakened me to the point that it was an effort to raise the weighty silver spoon to sup from it. Once the dish was half-empty, I wanted to give up, but waste was worse than gluttony and so I persisted.

A crack of thunder startled me and I had barely recovered when a missile of some sort struck the window. The spoon was halfway to my mouth and when I dropped it in shock, it fractured the porcelain so the remaining broth seeped onto the linen.

'What is going on, girl?' Father rang his bell furiously, and Green ran in, eager to do his bidding.

'I have no idea,' I said, leaving the table to stand at the window and stare out at the sky, 'but it is an evil portent, being so black outside when it is not yet night.'

'I was not referring to the weather, Patience. It is

prematurely dark on account of the hailstorm. I was referring to the ruined crockery.'

'The sudden noise scared me, Father. As you are aware, I have a nervous temperament.'

He did not reply and simply clamped his lips together whilst Green waited on him, dabbing and mopping at my spilt broth, and no doubt eavesdropping.

A thought occurred to me. 'Father, where is Earnest?' He had not yet returned from interrogating Rose Driver. 'Are you not worried for his welfare?'

'As your brother is due to set sail on a warship in a matter of weeks, I expect he will survive a walk to the bottom of the valley and back, however inclement the weather.'

Earnest was entirely the wrong person to send on a mission to gather more information about my encounter, but just because he was about to become a naval chaplain, Father viewed him as some kind of warrior. In reality, I was the only Leaton twin in possession of any backbone, so my father should have permitted me to finish what I had started, or at least gone to investigate for himself.

The sky was far more ominous than warranted by hailstones. It could be no coincidence so soon after I had witnessed a ritual slaughter.

'Father, I am troubled that Earnest is out in this. Something terrible is about to befall him. Look at that sky!'

Hailstones the size of turnips crashed to earth and piled up. They pounded the roof and walls in similar fashion and when one hit the window, a pane of glass splintered. Here, at last, was Armageddon, and I got to my knees, clasped my hands and began to pray.

'O, God. Spare us, your pitiful children. A dark hand moves against us. The devil's disciple has called him to our door. Lord, please keep us and preserve us. Amen.'

I turned my eyes up to heaven. The witch would not

stop until her evil master had smashed our home to firewood.

'Madam,' yelled Green, 'get away from the window!'

But her warning came too late. Another pane shattered beside me and a shard of glass embedded itself in my cheek. I screamed and began to pray harder.

'It is nothing more than a hailstorm,' said my father. 'A bad one, granted. Come away from that window and let us tend your wound.'

When I made no move, Father and Green seized an arm each and dragged me to safety, pressing me into my chair. A drop of blood trickled from me and spotted the white cloth. I almost swooned at the sight but they propped me up.

'Spinster Green, I will remove the glass,' said my father. 'Prepare yourself with a napkin and when I say the word, press it firmly to my daughter's face. Are you ready?'

'Aye, Minister Leaton. Ready.'

Immediately, I felt a sharp sting and a gush of hot blood followed by a dull pain as Green applied the napkin to my wound. I closed my eyes and concentrated on praying. My father was too passive, and the devil and his minion would take full advantage of him. If he would not protect himself, then I would have to do it for him.

Even though I was at death's door, I prayed for the wellbeing of Earnest in this menacing weather and for his safe return, hopefully with his soul intact. Every time a Leaton attempted to intercede with a Driver, a malevolent force came between us and them. That godless woman had sacrificed an innocent lamb in an unholy pact and she had raised a storm against me and almost put me in my grave. And to think I had considered her a suitable match for my brother. Well, no more.

The Silver Spoon

ROSE

The hail fell for a couple of hours and by the time it stopped, the sky was too dark to send my visitor home. After that regrettable kiss, I'd held Earnest at bay till he grew tired of his pursuit and lay down. Now, he slumbered peacefully in my bed.

My bodice and kirtle were not yet dry, but I put them on, along with my boots, as if they would somehow bolster my resolve. I'd not dared sleep and perched on the cracket, watching Earnest as he slept, wondering at his newly shadowed jaw and chin, eyelids occasionally twitching. It would have been so easy to give in to him. It wasn't fear of losing my reputation that gave me strength, nor fear of Da's wrath, but fear of childbirth. Still, I couldn't resist and crept over to kiss him on the corner of his mouth, watching his lips curve and his eyes twitch as he came to.

'Earnest, it's morning. Time to go.' He grunted and turned on his side so I nudged him. 'You must wake up. I have to find my flock.'

More importantly, I had to get rid of him. A storm this bad made it more likely that my father would come by, and if he found Earnest, his life would not be worth living.

'You must leave. Someone might see you. Da is almost

bound to turn up, and if he catches you...' He wouldn't care that Earnest had only stayed here to avoid danger and would kill him, and maybe also me.

He woke with a start, opened one eye and didn't recognise me for a moment. 'But it's barely light,' he grumbled.

'Getting lighter by the second. Go home, please. Your father might be worried and mine could turn up at any time.'

The mention of his father failed to spur him on but when Barebones began barking, he scrambled to his feet. The collie sat at the door, alert.

'Someone's coming,' I hissed. 'Hide under the bed.' It was someone known to me or the dog would be growling instead. 'Quick, and not so much as a sneeze out of you.' I flung his cloak and boots after him, then trailed the quilt over the side of the bed. There was a loud knock.

'Rosie, it's your Da. Are you in one piece? I've fetched some more bait. If you're decent, lift the latch.'

'Coming, Da. Just a minute.'

I had a final glance around while I composed myself. When I opened the door, the moorland was scattered with translucent balls like big penkers. Da wasn't there but he'd left the sack of provisions on the step and shinned up the ladder on the side of the hut to inspect the roof.

'Have you seen this out here, Rosie? Did you sleep through it?'

'No, not a wink, and that's why I overslept this morning.' I was glad he was on the roof and couldn't see me blush at the lie.

Inspection complete, he grunted his approval and climbed down. Once over, he'd have jumped down. He was getting old. Still as broad as ever, but his springy black curls were streaked with silver.

'Barely a spelk out of place,' he said. 'Mark of good workmanship, that.'

'Of course.' My father always praised his own work and did it with no shame. He pushed a foot against a pile of glassy spheres.

'You're very flushed, lass. Not feverish, are you?'

'Mebbes a bit. I got very cold and wet yesterday.'

'Well, the weather's set fair the day, so you'll sharp recover. You get going and I'll stow these for you.' He picked up the sack and went into the hut, and I felt sick.

There was no way of leaving Da behind with a man under the bed because I'd not put it past him to search the hut just for the sake of it. Barebones wasn't helping by lying with her muzzle under the trailing quilt. I'd have to move her before my father wondered what she was pointing at.

'Da! Please don't trouble yourself.'

My voice was too high, and my face was on fire.

'Rosie, what's wrong? You're not yourself and even the dog's out of fettle. What's up, Barebones? Have you lost your bone under the bed?'

'Naught's wrong with me,' I said, far too quickly, 'and the dog's unsettled by the weird weather, that's all. Come on, lass, out of there.' The collie snorted and I hauled her up so she was sitting. 'I'm sorry you've had to brave the elements at this hour to check on me, Da. There's no need for you to do any more. Rest awhile and let me take care of everything. The ewes can wait a bit longer.' I forced a smile. 'In any case, would the best farmer in the dale bypass my flock without running an eye over them?'

I held my breath and almost collapsed when he grinned.

'Aye, you know me too well. They're all up on the high ridge waiting for some sunshine. Twenty-four ewes, a lamb and a cade. Take it you lost one?' When I nodded, he went on. 'Aye, they're not shifting anytime soon, so we'll have a devil of a job ticing them down again.'

He sat on the bed and took his ease while I put away the new stores, keeping my back to him, knowing my complexion would have me hanged one of these days. I only hoped that Earnest could keep still and quiet for as long as it took. I couldn't bear to sit down and busied myself doing nothing rather than face my father. But he wasn't an easy man to fool and he knew something was amiss.

'What's going on, Rosie?' He narrowed his eyes. 'What are you hiding?'

'Nothing. Just a bit tired, that's all.' I could hardly breathe and the walls were too close together to contain my father's temper. One slip by me and he might raise the quilt and reveal Earnest's hiding place, and there would be murder done before the day was out.

Unexpectedly, he laughed. 'Getting ideas above your station, are you, eating with a silver spoon like a fine lady?'

My eye fell on the other bowl. It was still on the floor, complete with spoon! How could I have been so careless?

'No, of course not.' I managed to laugh. 'Must have picked it up by mistake along with my provisions and as it was here I forgot myself and used it.'

Earnest must have left it when he put his bowl down. What on earth would I be doing with a silver spoon up here? Da picked it up and rubbed it on his shirt.

'I'll put it back in the drawer, sharpish. Your granny counts the good cutlery every Friday when she polishes it, and if she finds out you've been in amongst her silver, she'll cut your hands off.' He eyed me closely. 'I never took you for a thief, Rosie.'

Relief surged through me, and I did my utmost to look ashamed. However horrible it was to be called a thief, it was much better than being known as a whore.

Da pocketed the spoon. How would I ever manage to return it to the manse, and what if Minister Leaton missed it in the meantime? I had to calm myself. For the time being, Da believed it was ours. Everything else could wait.

Happy after solving the mystery of my odd behaviour, Da booted the door open. 'It's long past first light so we'd best get up the ridge and fetch those daft ewes of yours.'

I smiled weakly and tied my cloak around me, hoping my heart would stand the strain till Da went away. He leapt from the top step and headed towards the high crags. They'd be treacherous to climb, but the hazardous ascent was preferable to staying another minute in the hut.

When we left, I tried to keep Da's attention to the front of us so Earnest could escape. It would only take the smallest sound to draw my father's keen ear. Luckily, he was too busy exclaiming at the hailstones piled up everywhere, gleaming with water as the rising sun started to catch them. They were already melting, but I was grateful to the curious creations for providing a useful distraction.

The Looking Glass

PATIENCE

Father had banished me to my room, concerned about my loss of blood, and encouraged me to rest. As if I needed any more rest! Instead, I would prepare for the forthcoming skirmish, whether physical or spiritual.

Although the hailstorm had ended, my twin was yet to return from investigating my dire encounter with Rose Driver. Because Father was ignorant of Earnest's earlier transgression with the Ely housekeeper, he was not perturbed by his absence, convinced that he had merely taken shelter with a kind parishioner.

Nestled in my candlelit chamber with Green, I sat at the dressing table and examined my reflection in the mirror. The shard had made quite a cut. Quarter of an inch to the right and I would have lost an eye. That was the witch's intent, and I should sink to my knees and thank God for thwarting her, but a scarred face was a minor consideration in the midst of a fight with the devil.

Because it was too dark to see my wound properly in the dressing-table mirror, our servant raised the small looking glass to let me examine it more closely. I took it from her and fondled its silver handle, turning it near the flame so it glittered and drew Green's eye.

The vain girl coveted the frippery and I had often caught her admiring herself in it. The hand-mirror had no value for any Leaton, and the Church would not mourn its loss if it bought information that would save innocent souls.

'Do you consider a hailstorm of this magnitude out of the ordinary?' I asked her.

'No, madam. We always have peculiar weather in these parts.'

'Even so,' I said, nudging the looking glass towards her, 'it is strange that I alone received an injury. Almost as if someone had sent the storm to punish me. Someone like Rose Driver, perhaps?'

Green ran a questioning finger over the embellished frame of the mirror. When I nodded, she tucked it inside her apron pocket.

'I want to please you, madam. Truly. But the Drivers have been so kind to me and our May.'

She had gone shy, peering up at me through her lashes, but now that I knew her price, it was easy enough to buy her again. The mirror had a matching silver brush and I told her to pick it up.

As she dressed my hair, Green had to be dreaming of how it would feel to run it through her lustrous locks instead of my wiry black thatch. I imagined the pleasure it would give her, smoothing the silver brush through her hair, and how much it would gleam after one hundred strokes every night. I put my hand over hers and took the brush from her.

'Try it yourself, Matilda. You have such beautiful hair.' Green was afraid, aware of crossing some line, and knew that once she'd crossed over, there could be no going back. She paused, uncertain, and I held my breath, wondering which way she would fall. Would she be loyal to the people she had known all her life, who had given her a home in the past, or would she be loyal to her new employers, who would do so in the future? 'Here,' I said, realising she needed a little more suasion. 'Let me help you.'

I pressed her into the chair and unwound her coif so her tresses tumbled down across her shoulders. I grasped a thick hank, close to the roots. It was heavy in my hand and I applied the brush, drawing it down the length of her hair to its tip, releasing a faint trace of violets. She closed her eyes and sighed. Encouraged, I picked up a second golden skein, raised it high from her scalp, dug the bristles deep into the underside and swept upwards so the girl fairly quivered beneath my fingers.

'So tell me,' I said, 'what you know about the Driver family.' I leant forwards and whispered to her. 'Have no fear, Matilda, for you are part of our household now and under our protection.'

She glanced behind her as if scared of being overheard. I chose not to speak. The girl was on the brink of unburdening herself and it would not do to startle her, so I held my tongue, heart thumping hard all the whilst. And then our servant revealed her secret.

§

Green's secret was not quite what I had hoped for, despite the high cost to procure it, but whilst insufficient to procure a conviction of witchcraft, it might take me a step further in that direction. Rose Driver was not Andrew Driver's daughter. Her mother had simply duped the wealthy farmer into marrying her when she had a bellyful of another man's child. In fact, Rose Driver's natural father was none other than our very own sexton, Thomas Verger. How had the slatternly woman deceived the dark-haired Driver when her child had such bright red hair? Still, the woman had paid for her deceit with her life and that of her son. Soon, it would be the turn of her daughter to pay.

Armed with this information, I sought Father as I had a

duty to inform him of the wickedness in our midst. He had been all too keen to dismiss me when I reported Rose Driver's vile act with the lamb and the subsequent storm-raising, making soothing noises about my febrile imagination. He could not dismiss so easily this intelligence from a trustworthy source, and he would have to heed me, but I needed to share this revelation cautiously because my father was already thin-skinned on the topic of witches.

Father was irritated at my interruption when I found him, so I adopted my most sincere expression. I had practised it since childhood and he could not resist it.

'Patience, please do not gurn so. If you wish to speak to me, you need only ask.'

Sometimes, he did not deserve my help, but when I revealed my latest discovery his brow furrowed and I knew he would take me seriously at last.

'This is troubling for you to hear, daughter, and it worries me that our servant would so readily fill your ears with such tales.' He removed the parish register from his desk and opened it to the lists of baptisms, marriages and funerals. 'Your sight is better than mine, so search for the girl's christening – if there was one – and for her parents' wedding.'

Over his shoulder, I pored over the historical entries, all written in the same hand, which had grown fainter as the years passed. The Reverend Foster had maintained this element of the register at least, and I soon located Rose Driver's baptism. Her parents were noted as Jane and Andrew Driver. The old priest must have been in his cups whilst chronicling the occasion for he'd smeared the ink, rendering the date illegible. On leafing backwards to find the marriage, the month was likewise smudged. Mutton Clog being a parish with such a small population meant there were not enough adjacent records to draw any further conclusions.

'Your deceitful predecessor has made it impossible to

calculate the period between the parents' marriage and the child's baptism.'

'That does appear to be the case,' said Father, 'but it is common enough practice amongst sympathetic clergy. For our purposes, the register clearly shows that the wedding took place prior to the baptism, and we can read the names of both parents. So, Rose Driver's birth is legitimate, and whilst her colouring does call into question her bloodline, we should not hold her responsible for that. It does trouble me that our sexton may have dubious morals. However, we should not make accusations without evidence, and Spinster Green's gossip does not count as evidence in my view, so you are not to say a word either to Verger or to the Drivers and especially not to Farmer Driver. Do you hear me, Patience? I forbid you to speak of this matter to anyone.'

More cowardice on Father's part. I came dangerously near to breaking the fifth commandment and snapped the register shut. If not prepared to interrogate the Drivers, then my father should be outside, berating Thomas Verger for bastardy. Green would not lie to me, of that I was certain, and she would be my faithful ally in the undoing of Rose Driver. For now, I would record her evidence in my journal and continue in my quest. Father might not appreciate my help presently, but he would thank me one day.

SUMMER

Midsummer Eve

ROSE

The longest day was here and the sweltering heat and hard work had left me bone weary, but at least the shearing was finished. Da and May would go to the Town Moor for their annual trip to the fair to sell the fleeces, examine the show animals and buy some prize specimens. A few neighbours from the dale were going. Farmer Johnson, with Henry Green for a hand, and some of the Carters and Wrights.

These past ten years or so, Da had stopped taking me and Tilly to the midsummer fair, complaining it was too rough and infested with cutpurses, vagabonds and footpads. According to him, it was no place for young women, yet he still took May, and everyone knew why. A woman as comely as my stepmother would be a draw. We had good wool, but so did most of the bishopric, leading to stiff competition, so he needed May to run the barrow and draw the eye of the merchants.

Once over, the whole family used to go, and if there was space on the wagon, Henry would join us. As a bairn, I'd loved to see all the sights, but once Granda died, we were all left behind. Although we missed the fair, we'd not been too badly off at home as there were always solstice revels here. Roaring bonfires, a spitted boar, mead, ale and merrymaking aplenty. But now Minister Leaton had banned all celebrations, other than those sanctioned by him.

A list had been nailed to the church door. Hardly anyone in the parish could read, but Tom Verger read it and told Blenkinsop, so word spread soon enough. All solstice festivities were banned completely. A harvest blessing would take place, but there'd be no harvest supper, no kern dolly or kern baby, and no fires. Christmas would be an opportunity to attend church thrice instead of once, but there'd be no Yule celebrations. Under sufferance, the farm machinery could be blessed on Plough Monday. At Candlemas, Minister Leaton would bless our candles on condition they weren't used for scrying. At Easter, pace eggs would be allowed, but neither rolling nor dunshing were permitted.

The news outraged the whole dale, who worried what cancelling the old celebrations might mean for our crops. The Beltane firewheel was the high point of the year, which nobody wanted to miss. The farmers were bent on going ahead with the usual purification and fertility rituals but the vicar got wind of their plans and his daughter had done the rounds, visiting every house in the parish – except ours – with threats of fines and excommunication. We were braced for our visit and Da had already warned us not to lift the latch to anyone if he was out.

When the knock finally came, Da answered the door himself. Outside stood Patience Leaton in her curious dark clothes and her prissy white pinny and collar. She was all alone and there was no sign of her father or brother. I hadn't seen Earnest since the hailstorm. He'd never come calling on me at the farmhouse, but I couldn't blame him when Da's fiery temper was widely known about.

The vicar's daughter carried with her the parish register and when Da barred her entry, she made a great show of reading from it. Her high voice wavered, full of self-importance.

'For failure to observe the sabbath for the past two

decades, a fine of some fifty pounds has been levied against this household. Adjusted for the premature–'

Da barked with laughter and shut the door in her face.

'Fifty pounds,' he said, leaning on the door, as if our unwanted visitor might burst through it.

Patience Leaton knocked again, and when no one opened the door, she called out.

'Adjusted for the premature demise of James Driver, and not including holy days other than Sunday. We have been most lenient, because the Church has failed in its duty of pastoral care by letting the debt climb so high in the first place.'

Da's shoulders shook with silent mirth. 'As if anyone north of the bishop's palace has that kind of money.'

'We do not mind how it is paid,' shouted the girl. 'If not in gold, we will gladly take your livestock, or even the farmstead.'

Granny got to her feet. 'Over my dead body will you take this steading, you thieving shrew. My late husband's family have held the tenancy since I don't know when. And now it's my widow-right. Church, indeed. I'd like to see you try and take it from me.'

'Do not test me, Widow Driver. I have God at my side. He is ever with us Leatons. Can the same be said of your family?' We never got a chance to reply as the girl answered her own question. 'God is not at your side, for how can He be when you give safe haven to a witch?'

At this, Da stopped laughing and he reared up, seeming almost twice his usual size. He flung open the door and ripped the register from Patience Leaton. The shocked girl squeaked and made to grab for it, but he held it above her head and tore it in two.

'Here, Ma,' said my father. 'Hoy this chaff on the fire.'

'Gladly,' said Granny, carrying out Da's request without blinking.

'You will not destroy God's word!' shouted Patience

Leaton, jabbing her finger at Da but cowering from him at the same time.

'That's not God's word, but the scribblings of old Reverend Foster. And all this mention of fines is just a plot to steal the earnings of honest working people. Go home and never set foot on our land again, Miss Leaton.'

The vicar's daughter stepped backwards, almost tripping over her own feet, but continued pointing at Da. 'You are mistaken, Farmer Driver. If you cross me, you cross God and it will go badly for you and yours. You may depend upon it.'

Da laughed and feinted at her and she fled in fright, clutching her skirts.

For all the farmers' fighting words, Beltane passed with no maypole, let alone a Queen of the May or a firewheel. There was joy in the ancient ways but celebrating in secret went against the spirit of it and the villagers soon lost heart. What right did this Leaton man have to make so many people so miserable? At Beltane, we'd had to content ourselves with standing on the brow of the hill, looking across to the Borders, where flames flickered in neighbouring parishes.

Summer solstice would pass us by without it being marked in any way. The sun would set and rise, with or without our thanks and praise, but it would be a sad day. I begged to go to the fair, but my father wouldn't hear a word of it so I had to content myself with seeing him and May off.

Once we'd finished loading the wool onto the wagon, Da took his seat and waited while May clambered up beside him. I wondered whether she would leave him now that Tilly was settled, and where she might go.

'Rosie, before you turn in, cast an eye over the livestock.

The cattle were late out to pasture this year and they're still settling themselves down. Then get yourself straight home.'

'Aye, Da. But after checking the livestock, I'm going to the old mill pond.'

'Fair enough, but home by dark. I don't want you out wandering in the middle of the night. Not on this particular night. Not with Leaton running the parish and that chit of his up on her high horse. And you know what your granny's like if she wakes up to an empty house.'

Granny clicked her tongue. 'Hadaway with you, Andrew. What's left in this life that can frighten me?'

But my grandmother hadn't been the same since Granda died, and she was nervy at night, so I promised to make sure she wasn't left on her own.

'You mind yourself, son,' said Granny. 'Not much can go wrong here in the valley, but the town's another matter.'

Da grunted and flicked the reins to set the horses cantering, and off they went along the low road to Newcastle.

❧

Granny was generally nodding in her chair by early evening, so after I'd helped her to bed, I let Barebones loose in the river. It felt mean to leave the dog behind, but my conscience would be clearer for not leaving Granny on her own. I packed some cheese and ale in my sack, and for a moment considered borrowing the household tinderbox to light a fire of my own, but smoke would draw the minister's eye. Resigned, I left it and picked up my crook.

After roaming the valley to check on the cattle, I climbed the hill to look over my sheep. Da's herd and my flock were all well, just grazing and enjoying the summer night, so I sat on the tops and watched the sun as it began its slide to the west. Over in the north, above the mountains of Scotland, a band of yellow glowed against the faint blue sky, which never grew truly dark at midsummer.

As far as my eye could see, fires burned in all the surrounding dales. Our neighbours, seeing out the light with eating, drinking, singing and dancing, as their vicars hadn't put paid to their celebrations. We were all sad when Reverend Foster died, but he was an old man and a tired one, so he was glad to go to his eternal rest. But if he'd known what would become of his beloved Mutton Clog, I daresay he'd have soldiered on for a few more years.

Summer solstice was always a lovely evening, but the minister had put an end to that. So, I'd mark the occasion by myself, swimming in the old mill pond beneath the dying sun, then sleeping with the starry sky as my mantle on this, the shortest night. Providing I got up with the sun, I'd be home long before Granny awoke.

I'd not so much as dipped a toe in the pond throughout May after all the icy melt water from April, but it was warm enough come June. It had been a blessing during the scorching hot days, though this summer hadn't been the same without Tilly. I'd scarcely clapped eyes on her since she'd gone to work at the manse. On her half-days, she'd visited and told us all about her new life. Although she didn't linger either time, my friend seemed happy enough and talked a lot about the Leatons and how she pitied the motherless twins. I'd been tempted to ask after Earnest but decided it was best not to say anything to Tilly now that she worked for his father.

I set off through the woods, drunk on the heady scent of fennel and woodbines, and kept climbing till I crested a small rise and entered a glade. There, the pond lay before me, wide and still, with blue and green dragonflies skimming the surface. The setting sun had stained the water so it shone like an old sovereign.

After lodging my sack in a shady nook, I untied my boots and peeled off my stockings, wriggling my bare toes in the grass while unfastening my clothes. Once free of my shift, I enjoyed the air on my skin. Around me, the birds sang unseen in the leafy trees, their songs sweetening the surrounding air, and I stretched, delighting in the sounds of the summer evening.

Slowly, I eased myself into the pond, lowering myself a little further with every step. Walking through the silt, I was soon in up to my neck. Now to leave the soft songs of frogs and grasshoppers, the gossiping birds and my sheep bleating in the distance. I arced forwards and swam underwater for a few yards before surfacing and pausing to wring out my hair and tie it in a knot. When I turned, it was to see Earnest Leaton standing at the water's edge, fiddling with my crook. He glanced at my clothing and lifted a brow.

'When I saw your clothes, I feared you drowned.'

'Simply washing away the heat of the day.'

'I might join you,' he said, shedding his puritan conscience as quickly as his snowy collar and stiff, black clothes. He untied his fine linen shirt and revealed his linings. It was hard not to laugh.

'Have you been sewn into your vest, Earnest Leaton?'

'Every Michaelmas since childhood. Smeared in goose fat, swaddled and stitched up.'

'For the sake of chastity?'

'Warmth, mainly. Chastity is an unhappy coincidence.'

He grasped the vest, ripped it at the seams and threw it down. The vicar's son was strong and sinewy for all he lifted no implement heavier than a pen. His foreskin was as delicate as the underbelly of a newborn lamb and only his hands and face had ever seen daylight, and then precious little of it, for his hide was white, apart from his chest, groin and calves where dark hairs grew. He picked his way towards me and slipped so he entered the pond suddenly and vanished beneath the water. When he emerged, his hair stood in a shock of black spikes. He gasped and coughed till he caught his breath, then rubbed his face and began wading in my direction, but soon ran out of floor and went under again. He spluttered to his feet and blundered towards me. As he neared, I ducked, twisting out of his reach. Watching him sink again, I considered rescuing him from a certain drowning, but when his hands clasped my waist from behind, I turned to face him.

Earnest regarded me. His eyes were hooded but he smiled. He had always seemed so buttoned up, but now his bare skin was touching mine. My heart was beating too fast and it was getting hard to breathe.

'It will take more than a layer of goose fat to deter me,' he said, silver eyes glinting.

With that, he drew me to him in a long embrace and I wrapped my legs about him, returning his kiss. The world was still, and despite the cold water, heat flared in me. I cried out and bit into his shoulder – hard – as he moved within me. As his pleasure mounted and reached crisis, he clasped me against him till I could scarcely breathe. He shuddered, then pushed me from him, gripping my upper arms so tightly they'd be bruised come morning.

At arm's length, my lover examined me. 'How did you make me do that?'

I laughed but it was a brittle sound. 'Make you do what?'

Earnest didn't laugh back. 'You understand perfectly what I mean.'

'I didn't make you do anything.'

'Yes, you did, temptress.' He traced my brow with his thumb. 'With your hair and your eyes and your skin.' He ran his thumb across my collarbone and down to my sternum. 'Get out and get dressed. Someone could see us.'

'And what if someone did see us?'

'If that someone was your father, he'd geld me.'

'Aye, he would, but he's a good knifeman and would make a clean job of it. Consider yourself lucky he's away in Newcastle so you're safe, for now.'

Earnest slapped at himself. 'Cursed midges. Eating me

alive. I must go and so should you. At least cover yourself. Anyone could pass by and see you. Or is that your game, lying naked in wait for unsuspecting youths?'

'You're no youth,' I said, 'and far from innocent.'

The sun still burnished our skin but my blood ran cold as the realisation of what I'd done sank in. Far worse than being ruined, I'd risked catching a bellyful.

As soon as my courses started, Granny and May had taught me how to reckon my fertile time according to the moon and they'd drummed into me the importance of avoiding men till I was married. They didn't need to tell me twice. Motherhood was the last thing on my mind so I'd never bothered to work it out. But now I had to make the effort. From memory, the moon was still waxing gibbous, so it wasn't quite my fertile time. To be on the safe side, as soon as May returned, I'd tell her and ask her to brew something for me. One of her awful juleps. It was a shame the lambing and calving were finished, or I could have seen to myself.

It seemed that the sight of me thinking also tempted Earnest from his godly ways and he lunged for me again. But I was sore now and had seen a different side to him, so I slipped underwater, intent on reaching the other side in a few swift strokes. He was too fast though, and caught me in an underwater embrace. On surfacing in his arms once more, I heard someone shouting but was too waterlogged to see or hear properly. I shook my head to clear the water and opened my eyes to find Patience and Tilly staring – open-mouthed – and the Leaton lass covered in clarts. Earnest let go of me immediately. I took a deep breath and sank to the bottom of the pond. How long had those two been standing there? What had they seen? And why was Tilly crying?

When my heart started pounding in my ears, I surfaced. Tilly and the two Leatons were gone. I continued to swim alone for a while, floating on my back and watching the dying sun glowing through the trees and bronzing their uppermost branches. Shivering, I clambered out and fell onto the warm grass, allowing the last rays to warm my skin as the water ran off me. The earth was warm and dry but the clear night would bring dew so I pulled my cloak over me.

As the sky finally darkened, the moon took the place of the sun, ready to keep watch over the earth for a few short hours. Rising above the trees, she revealed herself in all her fat glory, silvering the pond and smiling down at the reflection of her round face. I put my hand on my belly, and my heart contracted. What had I done?

Fornication

PATIENCE

On midsummer eve, my brother had been in a state of agitation all day, pacing beside the window to the west. He had his eye on a silhouette on the hill opposite. The witch, of course. Who else would be defiant enough to watch the sun setting on the longest day when celebrations had been forbidden?

The sultry weather was already a trial and we had no need for the added excitement of nocturnal festivities. These heathen festivals were blasphemous and led to an overflow of lust so it pleased me that Father had banned them, although it had taken a considerable amount of time and effort on my part to convince him of the need. In the end, I had written the list for him so he only had to sign his name to it. The sexton nailed the list to the church door for me, but he was visibly unhappy about it, and I confessed to being surprised that someone had taken the trouble to teach a gravedigger to read.

When Earnest slipped out, obviously intent on following Rose Driver, I decided to save him from himself, even if finding my way to the other side of the river would be challenging in the fading light. The valley was now smothered with dense, green woodland so the river only made itself known by its incessant rushing and by the occasional winding ghost of fog that sometimes undulated above the trees after rain on warm summer nights.

'Green,' I thundered. 'Come here, we have an errand to run.'

The flustered girl arrived in her nightgown and listened to my requirements.

'But, madam, it'll be dark in a few hours and it won't be safe to be out and about in the woods.' She crept closer to me. 'And especially not on solstice eve.'

I had to grip my right hand with my left to prevent myself from slapping our superstitious servant. 'God will keep us quite safe on our travels. Make yourself decent unless you wish to traverse the dale in your nightgown.'

The reluctant girl knew better than to disobey and soon reappeared in her dark frock, which still clung to her. Our scant fare meant there was much less of her these days, and a garment so old would not shrink unless it had been boiled. O, boundless vanity! The minx had taken it in. Tomorrow, she would let out the seams again, under my close supervision. The incessant heat in this house was already unbearable without adding further temptation.

'Have you any stouter shoes, madam?'

'These are my sole pair and sufficiently stout, thank you.'

Navigation at dusk was difficult and made more so by the overgrown bracken and stinging nettles. A less ardent Christian would have returned to the comfort of her chamber. The fading light made it difficult to see but I could just about discern my brother striding up the opposite hill. As he climbed, the object of his lust stood up, stretched and disappeared.

'Hurry, Green. We must not let my brother out of our sight.'

'There's no time to reach the ford then, so we'd better plodge straight through the river. Mind yourself on the bank, it's clarty here.'

This quaint word did not begin to describe the sucking bog I found myself in and it took the shoe right off my foot, causing me to step barefoot into soft mud.

'You may as well take them both off till we get to yon side, madam.'

The servant tied my shoes together and draped them around her neck, along with her own. With not a word of warning, she raised her hem to waist height, revealing a very round and bare behind. She glanced at me over her shoulder.

'Lift your skirts, madam. It's alright – there's no one here to see anything immodest.'

The naive girl did not realise my own modesty was not what concerned me. What had possessed me to venture into the woods at night, with their oppressive heat, their intoxicating perfume, the birds singing and this infernal girl half-naked in front of me. I prayed for deliverance from temptation and raised my skirts. The cold water extinguished the fire in my loins, and I would have stayed in the river for penitence were my brother's soul not in peril. But watching our servant's rump as she scaled the riverbank reminded me that my soul was also in peril so I turned my head until she covered herself.

'Come on, madam, or we're going to lose Master Leaton.'

The thought of parading my lower parts before a servant thrilled and sickened me in equal measure. Better to suffer wet clothing and the inevitable chill than to risk any more unseemly behaviour, so I let go of my skirts and the current caught them, almost sweeping me away.

'Oh, madam. I'll come and get you.'

With that, she hoisted her skirts again. O, the devil was abroad tonight, of that, there could be no mistake.

'Green! Stay where you are. God is my protector, and He will see me safely to the other side.'

I put my head down and thrashed to the opposite bank.

Were Green to hold out her hand, she might tempt me to pull her under, and then all would be lost.

Secure on the opposite riverbank, I collapsed, no longer caring about the mud. Mercifully, I had been delivered, free of sin, but on our return journey, I would insist on travelling first.

'Are you certain we are on the correct route?' I asked. 'Because this walk is taking an inordinate amount of time and Earnest vanished from sight long ago.'

'Don't worry, madam. He's bound to be heading for the old mill pond. There's not much else over that way. He'll be going for a swim, most likely. Me and Rosie used to go there all the time in summer.'

We progressed up the steep rise by dint of snatching at the thick woodbines snaking around tree-trunks. Near the top, Green put a finger to her lips and I paused to catch my breath. It would not do to arrive puffing and panting. Together, we crested the rise and Green clenched my arm so hard her nails almost broke my skin.

I followed her gaze to the large pond, where the two sinners emerged from the water in a tangle of arms. As naked as if they were in Eden, the pair of them. A fact brought home to me by the two piles of clothing shed nearby.

The servant was hurting my arm so I prised her fingers free, surprised to see her weeping. I had not thought her so sensitive to sin. There was hope for her yet, which was more than could be said for the two fornicators. Christian duty required me to rebuke them, but I dithered for too long and Green deprived me of the opportunity.

'How could you, Earnest?' she shrieked. 'How could you?'

Her cry alerted the fornicators, who shook their heads and rubbed water from their eyes. Their shocked expressions made me forget to reprimand our servant about addressing her betters in such familiar tones. Rose

Driver slid beneath the surface, leaving my brother to respond.

'Tilly? I mean Matilda. I mean Green. And Patience. What the devil brings you here?'

'God brought us here, Earnest, although too late by the looks of it.' I had seen enough and turned my back, encouraging our servant to do likewise. 'I will return to the manse and pray for your sullied soul, to say nothing of your ruined reputation. You will make yourself decent and pray for forgiveness.'

I seized Green by the arm and steered her back the way we had come. For all her capable navigation earlier, the talent was lost to her now and she was in some kind of reverie, and little wonder after beholding such lurid behaviour by her employer and her old bedmate.

Tidings of this improper behaviour would steal my poor father's sleep from him, so this secret would rest with me and Green. Earnest was not chaste, thanks to the wiles of our housekeeper in Ely, and the upset of keeping that secret had exacted a terrible toll on me. First, he had fallen prey to a wicked older woman but now he had fallen to a younger hag. These witches must sense in him the weakness inherited from our mother. I would pray for my brother, that he would soon go away to sea and be free from these terrible temptations. And then I would deal with Rose Driver.

※

It was close to daybreak when I tottered through the lych gate after Green. Our shoes and frocks were caked in mud and we abandoned them at the scullery door, creeping up the stairs in the half-light. Green put me straight to bed, and such was my suffering that I permitted her to pet me and pat me to sleep. I knew no more until a faint tap at the door disturbed me.

'Madam, are you awake?'

'I am now. What is it?'

The door opened and Green shuffled in, still wearing her nightdress.

'It's gone eight o'clock. Your father found me asleep and all but dragged me out of bed. He was in such a fury, but don't worry, he doesn't know why I overslept.'

Yet again, her face was tear-stained. Never had I known anyone cry so often or so copiously.

'My father will calm down. Sloth is a forgiveable sin so there is no need to take on so.'

She shook her head vigorously. 'That's not why I'm crying.'

'Has Father somehow learned of last night's events?'

The servant forgot herself and actually perched on my bed.

'Oh, madam, our May's husband is dead.'

'Dead? Andrew Driver?'

'Aye. Farmer Johnson came up early on to see about the funeral. In a state, he was, even though Andrew Driver's a bad man. Was a bad man.'

I got up and went to the window. Below me, the sexton was already digging a grave, although he'd barely dug three feet down. The day was not yet too warm, but by eleven, he would have to remove his shirt.

'Are you certain Driver is dead? He strikes me as an unusually robust man.'

'Aye, he is that. Was that.' She wiped her eyes on her sleeve. 'He never could keep his fists to himself. But that's not what's been the death of him.'

It transpired that Driver had been killed by a wool merchant he had cuckolded, but our servant got no further and lost herself to a paroxysm of weeping. Really, she was a most unsatisfactory source of information and the sexton might be more conversant with the facts. Quickly, I dressed and checked my complexion for smuts and my hair for brambles. Even on such a day, it was important to maintain a sense of propriety. By the time I arrived in the churchyard, the sexton was four feet down and heaving out slabs of slimy, wet clay.

'Mr Verger?'

'Aye,' said the impudent sexton, failing either to look up or pause in his labour. 'What can I do for you?'

'You can stop digging for a start.'

Wearily, he pushed his spade into the earth and leant on it. 'I need to get on. What do you want?'

'This pit,' I said. 'Who is it for?'

He wiped the back of his hand across his brow and left a smear of grave dirt across his forehead. I had the uncanniest urge to lean down and wipe it away.

'It's for Driver.'

So Green was right. 'What happened to him?'

'Something that's been long overdue, if you ask me.'

That our sexton would speak ill of the dead, and whilst preparing his place of rest, was an unacceptable lapse in decency.

'Tell me what happened, but be mindful of whose grave you dig.'

'Driver was stealing other men's goodwives, as usual, but he picked on the wrong fellow for a change. I've been on the receiving end of him once or twice meself, and he took some beating. But the merchant must've known that and armed himself.'

'Will they hang the merchant for murder?'

'Doubtful.' He shrugged. 'Classed as a revenge-killing, by all accounts. No law against it for a cuckold. Farmer Johnson had to drive May home, as well as her husband's corpse. Poor lass, getting caught up in the thick of it.'

He shook his head and resumed digging, leaving me no choice but to return to the manse. All the way, I could not help picturing Driver's corpse resting on a door after being laid out by his wife and mother.

Farmer Johnson, who appeared otherwise quite blameless, had pled on behalf of the bereft family, asking for a service and burial. A church service was out of the question but the dead man would be buried beside his father and sister. Given the family's history of non-observance, this was quite a dispensation from Father.

I was not sorry the lawless man was dead and would have left him in Newcastle to rot after his treatment of the parish register. More importantly, Rose Driver had lost her chief protector, which would make my coming task easier. It could wait until after the funeral, though. As a good Christian, I would permit her to mourn her father. But not for too long.

Loss of Consortium

ROSE

It was still half-dark as I wandered home from the old mill pond on the morning of Midsummer Day, but on reaching the brow of the hill, I saw lights glowing in our windows. Granny! What had happened to her? I ran straight down to the farmstead. My grandmother was hunched in her chair, weeping as I'd never seen her weep. May sat with an arm around her, shushing her as if she were a colicky infant.

'Oh, Rose,' wailed Granny. 'Thank God. There you are.'

May beckoned me over to sit next to her and put her free arm around me.

'Where's Da?' I asked. At this, Granny wailed louder.

'Something's happened,' said May. 'I'm very sorry, hinny.'

'What? What's happened to my father?'

Granny's head jerked up. 'He's dead is what's happened. And you out wayfaring without a care in the world and me fast asleep in my bed. Oh, it's more than I can stand.'

Dead? How could Da be dead when he was so strong and never sick? I huddled into myself, shivering. May got up, draped me in a blanket and hugged me again. Barebones sat at my feet with her chin on my knee, whining softly. Da was bad – I knew that, and my stepmother knew it most of all – but he was still my father and I loved him for good or ill.

Gradually, I managed to take it in and learned that some Newcastle wool merchant had accused my father of stealing his goodwife. The merchant had gone to the fair armed with a cudgel. He'd taken Da by surprise when he was standing on the wagon so he fell backwards and landed badly, breaking his neck. May patted my hand, promising me that it was quick and that he'd have felt naught, as if that would comfort me.

'But the killer can't be allowed to get away with murder,' I said. 'Can he?'

'The sergeants said there was no murder. They reckoned it's lawful for one man to kill another who's taken up with his goodwife because it deprives him of... what did the sergeants call it? Loss of consortium. Whatever that means.'

❦

Always a kindly man, Farmer Johnson had fetched home my father, his horses and his new widow. When my grandmother recovered herself, she began blaming May for not being properly upset.

'It's not natural for a woman so recently widowed. She should be in no fit state for anything, like me. And it was very convenient for Johnson to be on hand.'

'Granny, he's our neighbour and it was good of him to help. He had to leave his own horse with Henry Green. What was May supposed to do – drive the wagon home herself when Da never let any of us take the reins? Without Farmer Johnson, we'd have no body to bury and we'd have lost the horses and all.'

'Cold comfort, that,' said Granny, but my words had hit home.

Nobody could blame my stepmother if she was relieved at Da's passing, but instead, she was silent. It must have terrified her, witnessing my father's murder, however badly he'd treated her. Wisely, May didn't say a bad word against him as my grandmother wouldn't take it too kindly and I no longer cared to dwell on his failings myself.

Together, my stepmother and grandmother laid his body out. Henry Green took a door off its hinges and Da lay in the parlour, surrounded by herbs and flowers picked from the kitchen garden. Being high summer, we had to have an early burial.

'In my day,' sniffed Granny, 'we'd have kept him in the dairy but folks these days don't think that's proper.'

Thanks to Farmer Johnson and his reasonable manners, the minister agreed to bury Da in the family plot. There was to be no church service, but there would be a short committal prayer.

My stepmother was being careful around my grandmother, almost as careful as she'd been around Da, and no wonder. As a young widow, she had no belongings to her name bar the clothes on her back. On Granda's death, Granny exercised her widow-right and took over the tenancy of the farm, but she'd refused to put it in her son's name, and he'd grumbled about being ruled by women in his own home.

Had Da got his way and the farm put in his name, May would now be the customary tenant and in a far happier position than the one she now occupied. Granny had suffered her all these years because she was married to her son. Now that May was widowed and her sister safe with the Leatons, I wondered what might become of her. But I had worries of my own and had already ignored them for too long, though it wouldn't be fair to ask my stepmother for help just yet. Besides, I was still hopeful that the chances of falling wrong on my first outing were small.

❧

Hardly anyone attended the funeral and I couldn't blame them when it had poured down for days on end after the hot weather brought thunderstorms and endless downpours. Minister Leaton and Tilly attended, but Earnest and his sister didn't show their faces. Farmer Johnson came, Mr Blenkinsop, and the rest of the Green family, along with a few farmers from the dale hoping for a free feed. The heavy rain pleased Granny.

'It's never right, burying someone on a sunny day. An insult to their life and no more. This is better weather for a burial.'

It wasn't better for Tom Verger and Henry Green, battling with the handcart, which kept getting stuck in the clarts. The church coffin was too narrow to fit Da's shoulders so Tom Verger built one especially. I was glad Da had some protection from the rain and wouldn't be carried to church in just a winding sheet on such a wet day.

It had taken me a while to summon the courage to sit in the parlour. I'd taken Da's hand, shocked at how cold it was against my own. He was devoid of colour and everything familiar in him had gone. He looked so peaceful now and I wondered why he'd always been such a harsh man. But it was too late to find out now as my father had taken all his secrets with him.

Granny led the small funeral procession up the hill, refusing all offers of assistance, chin raised in the teeming rain. When we entered the lych gate, we rested while my grandmother caught her breath. Minister Leaton was sheltering in the vestry doorway and showed no sign of leaving, even once we'd assembled at the graveside.

Together, Tom Verger and Henry Green placed Da's coffin on top of two ropes, which they then threaded through its handles. To the foot of the grave lay an enormous heap of clay. Staring down into the pit made my knees weak. It was so deep and dark and cold looking, with the bottom drowned in muddy water. Worms and slugs crawled on the clay walls and I hated the thought of my father being put into earth that was wet and solid and infested with slithering creatures. I leant my head on May's shoulder and she rested her head against mine. At least Da was snug in oak lined with soft wool, which would keep him warm and dry for a time.

Granny stood facing the vestry. 'Well, we cannot very well have a burial if the minister won't leave his station.'

I smiled despite myself, glad to see a bit of her old fire again. But Minister Leaton was not to be moved and began to recite his prayer without leaving the shelter of the vestry gable or raising his eyes from the prayer book, concentrating on the page as if it were the first time he'd uttered the prayer of committal.

'We have entrusted our brother Andrew to God's mercy,' he droned, 'and we commit his mortal remains to the ground. Earth to earth...'

On hearing these words, Granny almost pitched forwards into the grave and Farmer Johnson clasped her to him as she grieved for the loss of her son. Tom Verger and Henry Green lowered the coffin slowly without making the slightest splash as it ended its short journey. My grandmother stooped to claw up a handful of clay and dropped it onto the oak, her face folding in on itself. Me and May threw a handful, then hurried to each side of Granny to take an arm.

'Come on, Bet,' said May. 'Let's get you home.'

'What's the point,' she cried, 'when I have no family any more?'

'You still have us,' I said. 'Me and May.'

'Oh, you and May. You and May. What earthly good are the pair of you?'

We glanced at each other. Granny wasn't herself, and losing her son was a terrible shock. Granda had suffered from a poorly heart all my life, so when the end came, it was sad but not sudden like this.

Friends and neighbours followed us home in the rain. It would comfort Granny to have a houseful of people for a few hours. She'd barely stopped weeping since hearing about Da and showed no sign of letting up. I hoped not to give her anything else to cry over.

۶۵

Within a fortnight, that hope was dashed. My courses were absent, there was a hardening in my belly and my breasts ached. According to the moon, my bleeding was due today so my fate was clear. I would give anything to undo what I'd done that night at the mill pond with a man barely known to me. There was no excuse for it, other than my good sense weakening in the arms of a man so pleasing to look at and full of wit, who'd set light to something inside me. A woman of a more superstitious bent might have blamed my behaviour on the solstice, but there was nothing and no one at fault but me.

Regardless of how or why it happened, Earnest hadn't come near me since, and no wonder when I'd already given him what he came for. Every night since Da's murder, my dreams were haunted by my mother and brother dying, and I'd woken up, suffocating in the stench of blood, sick with fear that this new life in my belly would be the finish of me.

Unable to look Granny in the eye, I spent as much time out of the house as possible, hoping to catch May on her own. I couldn't tell her my news in the house for fear of being overheard. Either way, she'd soon know on laundry day when there was no bloody linen from me. I sat on the steps of the shepherd's hut and stared across the valley, hoping to spot my stepmother alone.

A while later, my heart lurched at the sight of Earnest running downhill to the river. I withdrew into the hut. If he was coming here, it wouldn't do for us to be seen together. Four people knew what took place on midsummer eve, but gossip spread faster than weeds in Mutton Clog. When he bounded up the steps and into the hut without knocking, he was grinning, flushed from the effort of running, his hair ruffled by the breeze.

'Might as well be hanged for a sheep as a lamb,' he said, as he cupped my left breast and drove me backwards onto the bed.

I caught his hand, shoved him off me and stood up.

'We should make haste,' he said. 'Patience has me all but under lock and key and will soon miss her prisoner if I fail to return in time for evening prayers.'

Again, he pushed me towards the bed and I stiffened, holding my ground.

'Rose, what's the matter?'

'We shouldn't be doing this,' I said. 'That's what's the matter.'

'You were happy enough at the pond, so what has changed?'

'Da's death, for one,' I said, twisting out of his grasp. 'But there's more–' I tried to bite off the words before they were out of my mouth, but he guessed immediately.

'My God. You are with child?' He scoffed. 'So you are determined to ruin me.'

'Ruin you? You've ruined yourself.'

What had I ever seen in Earnest Leaton when he had no care for me but only for himself?

'How can I be certain the bastard is mine?'

These words were like ice in my heart. 'Of course the child is yours. There's been nobody else.'

'So you say. How can I accept your word? The word of a girl who will lie with a man she barely knows is worth very little, for she will no doubt lie with anyone.'

'That's not true, Earnest, and it's cruel of you to say so.'

Had I ever known him at all? He looked more like a stranger with every minute that passed and I was determined he would not see my fear.

'You are a wanton so I cannot believe I was your first.'

'But I bled.'

He shrugged. 'I have only your word for that, and as we already know, it is not worth so very much. Regardless of who fathered this child, I will not permit you to give birth, not when there is my name to think of, and my future wife and family. There are ways and means. So you must rid yourself of your burden.'

I almost choked at this. '*My* burden? It's as much yours as mine. You are not who I thought you were, Earnest Leaton. Do you realise what you condemn me to?'

'You condemned yourself, Rose. I did not force you.'

He swallowed and the Adam's apple bobbed in his throat. I'd thought him handsome and fine with a clever mind. He was a man when he took me in his arms, but now, he had the sulky mouth of a petulant boy afraid to step out from the long shadow of his father and the Church. I couldn't bear the sight of him. Why had I given myself to him so freely? He had no concern for me, but only for his reputation. He'd made himself appear sweet so he could use me. Why had I been so unwary? But if naught else, we were of one mind, and he would not expect me to bear his child. For that alone, I was grateful.

Jezebel

PATIENCE

Immediately after breaking my fast, I went upstairs and sat in the window seat of my chamber. There, I observed Thomas Verger at his work, which involved nothing more exerting than weeding the churchyard. At last it had stopped raining and the sun shone, but he laboured beneath the shade of a leafy oak so his shirt was still on his back. That would almost certainly change if he did any digging, for the man could barely dig four feet down before his shirt would be off and tossed over a nearby gravestone.

Disconcertingly, I had competition in this regard, more than once catching Green idling by my window, wearing a foolish expression. I warned her she would be sacked and sent home if caught in dereliction of her duties again, but since the occurrence at the pond, she had meekly gone about her labours, giving me no further cause to scold her.

Unfortunately, apart from Andrew Driver, no other parishioner had died recently, so there would be no more graves to dig. Unlike Ely, where the arrival of summer brought with it fen fever, as soon as the sun came out here, everyone's humours vastly improved and it looked as though I would have to wait for winter again, unless there was an accident or another act of violence.

At present, the sexton was shoring up some crooked gravestones, his shoulders straining with the exertion. The man had stolen some of the scented white roses rambling up the front wall of the manse, and as he replaced each stone, he put a flower on the grave. Did the man not care what commandments he broke? Little wonder his natural daughter was so iniquitous. But disciplining the sexton would have to wait because I was too worried about my twin. A letter had arrived for him earlier, but he had not shared his news and was doing his utmost to avoid me.

Below, the front door opened and Earnest emerged, walking through the graveyard without passing the time of day with Verger. Instead, he set off down to the valley at a fair clip. In recent weeks, he had not been himself, perhaps unsettled by guilt. Sick with shame, he could look neither me nor our servant in the eye. I was not myself either, whiling away the hours watching a plebeian man when I could be improving my soul or updating my journal. It was just as well Green kept to herself. Such were the temptations of Mutton Clog that I must stiffen my resolve. A purge or some such would restore me to my right temper, but I could trust no person in this parish with such an intimate task.

Within a couple of hours, my brother returned and crossed the graveyard, head down, walking uncommonly fast until he stalked into the house, slamming the door behind him. This was most unlike him and I determined to uncover the cause of his upset. I found my twin in the parlour, pacing on the rug, picking up books and putting them down, opening his mouth as if to speak and then stopping himself. To prevent his agitation from affecting me, I picked up Father's Bible and set it down again, carefully squaring its edges with the corner of his desk.

'What troubles you, brother?'

He stared into the fire, unhearing, so I raised my voice.

'Does shame weigh on you after your latest debauchery?'

Earnest's head jerked upright. 'Of course not. It was an unguarded moment, and God knows I am no fornicator, but just an innocent weakened in the face of severe provocation. Now, I have learnt that the Jezebel is with child.' He took in a breath so long that it almost choked him and brandished some papers with broken seals. 'And today of all days, when I have received my naval orders.'

His anguish touched me so much that I crossed the room and pressed a hand to his arm. My feckless brother had exposed us to the witch's influence, but he was not to blame for foundering under the weight of Rose Driver's insidious wiles.

'You can rely upon me to help, Earnest. As I helped you once before.'

He shrugged off my hand and continued his pacing.

'That is no good. You finished off the housekeeper as well as her little problem. You went too far, Patience. Now leave me alone to think.'

I had not gone far enough. Not content with seducing my brother, our Ely housekeeper had brought me to the brink of death more than once, and as the sergeants finally carted her off, I was confined to bed, weak and delirious. Even from my sickbed, the devious hag could be heard protesting that I suffered from a simple case of fen fever and no more. As if I could contract such an ailment when I never frequented the marshes, drained or otherwise.

That foul servant kept a tame white mouse in a wooden hutch in the scullery. More than once I had disturbed her, crooning to the creature and petting it with a forefinger. The careless authorities left the rodent behind, and no witch could be put to death whilst her familiar lived. Despite being on the brink of death, I dragged myself from my sickbed and laced up my stoutest shoes. Praying loudly, I stomped the impish creature to death and burnt it on the kitchen fire, to the muffled horror of our old cook, who knew better than to cross me.

And now, here we were once again at the same juncture. Everything made sense to me now and all that remained was to convince my brother and my father.

'Earnest, I know you will not want to believe this, but please hear me out.' He rolled his eyes but did not otherwise object, so I continued. 'Rose Driver ritually slaughtered a lamb and raised a storm to kill me and leave you unprotected.' At this, he snorted in derision but I hurried on. 'Her spell-casting was designed to seduce you and get a child so she might use its innocent soul for her own dark ends. Corrupting a man of God must add potency to her evil plot, and since Father is beyond reproach, she went after you, an infinitely weaker vessel.'

'So says my hare-brained sister,' said Earnest, throwing his hands in the air. 'Will you listen to yourself? Spells and storms and seduction. Let me tell you, Rose Driver needs no midsummer magic to draw a man to her. You live in a world of dreams, Patience, whilst the rest of us have to live in the real world with all its problems.'

'If you do not require my assistance with your latest conundrum, brother, then you have only to say so. You are a resourceful man, so you may find your own solution, but if we are to be reinstated in Ely, we can bear not another whit of shame, so you must do something and you must do it before Rose Driver begins to show.'

'Patience,' said my father from behind me, 'fetch your brother some warm milk. He looks in want of sustenance.'

I whirled around to see Father standing in the doorway.

'Let me ring for Green,' I said, seizing the handbell.

'Obey me, girl,' he said, pointing to the door. 'Do not make me tell you again.'

He wanted rid of me so he could talk to my brother alone, which frustrated me, but for once there was no need to eavesdrop. Father finding out about the illicit child was not my primary concern. What my mother had done to our family's standing would pale to insignificance beside an act of bastardy by an ordained priest. Earnest had been a student the first time and that sin might have been forgiven had he been found out, but if the Church knew about this breach of canon law, he'd be stripped of even his humble naval chaplaincy.

The Driver woman had cast her spell starting that day with the sacrifice of the lamb, and now she had corrupted a young priest, imagining him pure. So it was Rose Driver who should be punished and her progeny dealt with. But I would not rush and repeat the errors made at Ely. I would take time to amass a proper body of evidence. The day of reckoning would come soon enough and I would ensure that Rose Driver was hanged by the court and not allowed to fade away gently like her predecessor.

When the milk was boiled, I poured it into a double-handled cup and returned to the parlour to find my menfolk deep in conversation. They spoke so quietly I could not hear anything. I coughed to announce my presence and passed the bowl into Earnest's hands.

'Congratulate your brother, Patience. He is to be married prior to taking up his chaplaincy, and we are pleased.'

These words gave lie to the expressions on both their faces. In particular, my brother looked as if he were going to his own funeral. That Father preferred him to marry a notorious sabbath-breaker, rather than tarnish his character, told me how concerned they both were for our family's remaining shred of honour. This mission in Mutton Clog represented our final chance to redeem the Leaton name, and if the existence of this illicit child was exposed, we would be cast out from the Church forever.

After making a great show of blowing on the milk, Earnest finally allowed himself a mouthful, but his dallying had allowed a skin to form, which now coated his lip. He gagged slightly, brushed it away and shoved the bowl into my hands.

'Have you forgotten that I detest a skin on milk, Patience? It sickens me. And you have boiled it so the smell alone is nauseating.'

I held the warm bowl and regarded my over-sensitive brother. My heart brimmed with pity. How would he ever survive having a wife and child, let alone offer solace to men sailing into war on foreign seas?

❦

Despite all attempts at suasion, the conjugal plan remained in place. Since Earnest's navy commission was imminent, Father promptly sent him in search of our paternal grandmother's wedding ring. I had grown up with the knowledge it would never belong to me because it was always destined for my brother's bride. I was to inherit my maternal grandmother's ring, but Granny Barker was so vigorous, she would easily outlive us all. Not that I had any need of a wedding ring, but the thought of Granny Leaton's sacred band encircling an unholy finger was intolerable. If my father knew the truth about the vile woman who would wear his mother's ring, he would surely have allowed her to be buried wearing it. I tried not to think of him wresting it from her cold fingers. It was incumbent upon me to prevent this false marriage from proceeding and attempt once more to confide my concerns. But I was out of favour with my father, not only because of Earnest but also due to my attempt to extract a fine of fifty pounds from the Drivers. On learning of my enterprise, he had expressed great displeasure and warned me not to interfere further.

Father's negligent approach to the sabbath-breakers left a good deal to be desired and his refusal to pursue the matter of their non-observance disappointed me. Since

Thomas Verger's election as churchwarden, he had not bothered to visit the non-observers and neither did Father pursue the matter with him. My father's reluctance to extract the dues owed surely resulted from the brawn and temper of Farmer Driver. Now that the farmer no longer presented a threat, I had urged Father again, but he would not hear of it, on the grounds of it being indecent to harangue the family when the man was barely cold in his grave and the household still in mourning. And now the heathen slattern was bearing his grandchild, he wanted to cause no trouble in that direction in case the woman refused Earnest. Granted, if she did reject his plight, it would go badly for her, being unmarried and with child, but it would go worse for my brother. Even so, I did not want this woman to marry into our family and there were other ways of resolving the problem. When my father seemed calm enough to be receptive, I made my approach.

'Father, I beg of you, please think again before you join your son to an unchristian woman.'

He blinked and his face hardened. 'The Drivers, or what's left of them, will come to church for the wedding. Once they revert to God, we will join together and become one family. Your brother's future reputation and living, and indeed my own reputation and living, are at stake here. We must put aside all other considerations and you must trust my judgement in this matter. Your brother *will* plight his troth to this woman, and we must pray she accepts him.'

No Better than a Bastard

ROSE

I was busy snipping Granny's hair while my stepmother swept up the cuttings and tossed them into the fire. Both of us were almost asleep on our feet. Late summer was the busiest time on the farm and we were struggling to keep it going. We had our regular hired help ready for harvest, but what would happen come blood moon and the slaughtering? For now, I couldn't think past what might dwell inside me. I needed to speak to my stepmother on her own, but since Da's death, my grandmother was glued to May's side all day. I tried to stay awake in the hope of speaking to my stepmother once Granny fell asleep, but it was hard to keep my eyes open lately.

'I'll have to cut your hair at waning moon, Granny, because it grows faster than I can cut it. Maybe I should leave you for when the shearer comes round next.'

'Aye, and he can see to you at the same time. You've a fair mop on you and all, Rosie.'

Her words held no malice but no smile either. Little wonder when she'd lost her daughter, her husband and her son, and I was all she had left to her. If I were a braver and better granddaughter, she'd have a great-grandchild to look forwards to, but I refused to sacrifice myself, regardless of her love for me.

I'd finished trimming May and was ready to start on myself when Barebones growled. A moment later, we heard a single knock. Someone was very sure of being obeyed. May answered the door, and there stood the vicar, flanked by Earnest and Patience. Dressed in their Sunday best, their strange garb made them look like a trio of magpies. Three for a wedding, according to the mart wives. Earnest would not meet my eye, instead rubbing his brow furiously, clearly wishing to be anywhere but here.

'Good evening, neighbours,' said Minister Leaton. 'Sorry to disturb you at this late hour but pray allow us to enter. My son has a question for you, Widow Driver.'

Granny stood up. 'Aye, have way. We can sit in the parlour and your daughter can busy herself with the two lasses. May, fetch in some whisky – a tot apiece – and we'll drink a toast to my late son.'

I doubted the vicar and his son drank but my grandmother enjoyed a tot so the visitors would raise a glass whether they liked it or not. The Leatons crossed the threshold and followed Granny, but she stuck out a hand and eased Patience Leaton towards us.

'Lasses to stay put, miss.'

The girl smoothed her white gloves as if she were a queen. 'As a guest in your home, Widow Driver, I cannot allow myself to be counted as a mere lass. Furthermore, in my mother's absence, I am mistress of the manse and deserve that much regard, so I am madam to you, not miss.'

Granny shifted to bar her path. 'I'm no spring chicken, miss, but I'm more than a match for a maid like you. Take a seat when you're told.'

I'd expected Patience to shove past, but she smiled primly and sat in Da's chair. Fortunately, Granny didn't see this. May followed with the whisky, and on her return, she hefted a pan onto the fire.

'Whisky's too strong for us, but a drop of spiced cider should do no harm.'

When she unstopped a crock and took a good pinch of spice, Patience Leaton leapt to her feet.

'No! Do not add any suspect herb. I will not touch it if you do. Even the possession of such condiments is highly suspect.'

May laughed but dusted her fingers clean and stopped up the crock again. 'As you wish. Plain cider it shall be.'

She ladled the warm cider into glass cups and passed them around. While we sat at the deal table, I worried about the discussions next door. Patience Leaton took a sip and winced, forcing a tiny smile.

'Most delicious, thank you.'

Just as well my grandmother wasn't here. Her cider was prized in the quarter and I'd tasted none better. Patience removed her gloves, arranging them neatly on the table.

'I wonder,' she began, 'where Rose gets her beautiful colouring from, given that Farmer Driver is – was – so dark.' She toed the pile of hair clippings. 'From her mother, perhaps? Her real mother, that is.'

'I take after my great-grandmother.' I looked at May. 'That's right, isn't it?'

'Aye,' she said, stiffly. 'That's right. On your mother's side.'

'How interesting,' said Patience. 'I suppose your mother's mother's mother...' she paused and rocked her head slightly from side to side as if counting to herself. 'I suppose that your mother's mother's mother must have been some relation to our sexton, since Thomas Verger has the exact same colouring as you.'

'You're much mistaken,' I said. 'The Vergers are no relation to the Drivers.'

Patience held up her cider, frowning as she turned it in the firelight. There was a smear on the glass and she put it down and pushed it away from her as if it were tainted.

'I am aware that the Vergers are no relation to the Drivers, but that is not what I asked.' She smirked at me, and May looked set to kill. 'My brother and father, poor innocents, are in your parlour asking for your hand in marriage. They have even fetched my late grandmother's gold ring for you.'

Her voice held a dangerous edge and I wondered what she was up to.

'But you are not fit to wear my grandmother's ring and you are not fit to be my brother's wife.'

So she'd found out about the child. I stared at her, willing her not to say any more, or they'd insist on me marrying and giving birth, and I'd be dead before the year was out, providing Granny didn't skin me alive first. Patience smiled at me. It was hard not to touch my belly so I nursed my cup to occupy my hands.

'Shall I tell you why you are not fit to marry my brother? Because you are no better than a bastard.'

At this terrible word, I gasped and dropped my cup. The glass shattered on the stone floor and soon fetched running footsteps. Whatever the Leaton lass was talking about, it was nonsense, but I had to avoid this offer of marriage.

'What the devil's going on in here?' Granny got there first, her face livid, fists clenched.

Patience Leaton buttoned up her gloves. She waited for her menfolk to arrive before answering.

'I was explaining how Rose Driver is not fit to be my brother's wife, because she is, in fact, no better than a bastard.'

She laughed, and it was a laugh both cruel and hollow. Granny's mouth opened but she didn't speak. In all my life, she'd never once been lost for words.

The Leaton lass went on. 'How ridiculous that the girl labours under the false impression that she is your granddaughter when Thomas Verger is her natural father.

Rose is descended from humble gravediggers – a most unclean occupation.'

I expected my grandmother to laugh and bundle Patience Leaton out of the house but she stood stock-still, the high colour now leached from her.

'Where did you learn this?' Granny demanded. Her voice was low and dangerous and I'd never heard her like this. She seized Patience by her snowy collar and shook her. 'Who told you this? Who?'

'Unhand my daughter at once.'

Minister Leaton was braver than his son, who concentrated hard on his shoes.

Granny let go of Patience – who flopped heavily back into Da's chair, clutching her throat – then turned on May, snarling.

'There's no need to ask who told her though, is there? Not when that bitch sister of yours shares their roof. God help me, when I get hold of your Tilly–'

'Stop!' I stood up, shaking. 'Stop this, all of you. What does it mean? Please, can someone tell me? Is Tom Verger my father? Is that what you're saying?'

Patience got to her feet. 'It means your loving mother had everyone foxed, but *mother* is too good a word for her, so let us call her by her proper name. *Whore*.'

Unable to stop myself, I slapped Patience. Her nose burst and blood gushed all over her collar and pinny. She rubbed at her nose then gazed at her hand, making no move to staunch the blood, but suddenly laughed and grabbed hold of my hair.

'Bet,' shouted May, 'I'll collar Miss Leaton and you grab Rose.'

Together, they dragged us apart. Granny hauled me into the parlour and sat me down, tut-tutting as she lifted handfuls of my hair.

'Look at the clip of you, Rosie. Red-faced and breathless, fighting like cats. So unruly. Let's start by taming this mane while you settle yourself down. If you're to wed a chaplain, you can't be carrying on like this.'

I bristled, slight pains firing up and down my neck and shoulders as she pulled hairs while weaving a tight plait.

'But is it true?' I blurted out. 'Am I the gravedigger's bastard?'

When her hands stilled on my scalp, anger pulsing through her fingers, it gave me all the answer I needed. The door opened and Patience Leaton appeared, followed by a harassed looking May and the Leaton men.

'You thought to coerce my brother into asking for your hand,' she snapped. 'Well, things have not quite gone to plan, Miss Driver, have they?'

'Marrying your brother is the last thing I'd ever want,' I shouted, not fully in control of myself.

'You Leatons had better leave my house,' said Granny. 'Go on, get. You're not welcome here. Rosie is worth ten of you and has no need of a Leaton ring on her finger.'

Patience smiled and laughed her hollow laugh again. I knew what was coming next and bowed my head.

'O, but that is where you are misguided, Goodwife Driver. Your *Rosie* is carrying my brother's child, so she has every need of a Leaton ring on her finger.'

My grandmother put down the brush and sank into her chair. 'Good God, lass. What are you trying to do to me?'

'I'm sorry, Granny. Truly and honestly sorry.'

I stared at my feet. My grandmother got up, put a finger under my chin and raised it so I had no choice but to look at her.

'The night of the hailstones. That damned silver spoon. I caught your da trying to sneak it into my cutlery drawer. I knew fine well it wasn't one of mine. I said at the time something was afoot. You were never a thief.'

'Not a thief, no,' said Patience Leaton, 'but certainly a whore. Like her mother.'

This time, I ignored her. Naught had happened on the

night of the hailstones, but it would serve no cause to correct Granny and tell her that my child was conceived the same night her son died. I wouldn't cry in sight of the Leatons. They wouldn't get that satisfaction when they'd shamed me in front of my family. Except they weren't my family. In the last hour, the world had shifted so it no longer felt steady beneath my feet, as if it might go reeling away at any minute. My grandmother had no reason to stand by me and nobody would blame her for disowning me. Instead, Granny thumped the table with her bony fist.

'There'll be no more bandying of sharp words in my home. So sit down, every last one of you. That includes all you Leatons.'

Granny stood with her arms folded. Even in her seventh decade, her shoulders remained square and her arms wiry. Beside her, the Leatons looked thin and frail. They might have God on their side, but he was not in this parlour and so they took their seats meekly.

'Until a minute ago, we were all settled that your Earnest would wed our Rosie. Granted, some of the facts were missing on both sides. First, you weren't aware that our Andrew raised the bairn as his own, even though she wasn't his.' Granny leant over the vicar, who cringed a little. 'The lass has done naught wrong, so this shouldn't be held against her. As to her having a bellyful, I've bred sheep all my born days, and it takes a tup and a ewe to make a lamb, and neither one of the two is any better or any worse than the other.'

Minister Leaton found his voice at last. 'Widow Driver, I think we are at cross-purposes. No one is suggesting for a second that Rose's paternity is at question.' Patience Leaton piped up but her father held up a finger in warning. 'We came here today to ask permission for Rose to marry Earnest. Nothing has changed. My daughter has admittedly stirred the pot and will be dealt with later. Like it or not, there is a child in the offing and as my son is due to sail as ship's chaplain in a matter of days, we must ensure this marriage proceeds with all haste. For that reason alone, I can dispense with the reading of the banns. Earnest and I will travel to Durham immediately to swear the bond necessary for a licence. In the meantime, my daughter and Spinster Green will act as bride's maids and remain at your granddaughter's side until the wedding.'

The thought of being taken prisoner in my own home terrified me, so before anyone could stop me, I dashed out of the house, past the barn and up to the church without stopping. I'd believe almost anything of Da but not a single word that spiteful girl said about my mother. I ran through the lych gate and into the graveyard, straight to my mother's grave and threw myself down on it, Barebones at my side.

After a while, I buried my wet face in the dog's fur and breathed her in till my heartbeat slowed. Those terrible lies couldn't be true. Calmer now, I ran my hand over the inscription on the cross. Reverend Foster had told me what it said and I had no reason not to believe him. *Jane Driver. Wife of Andrew Driver. Mother of Rose and James Driver.* What had happened? How could I possibly be someone else's daughter?

A long shadow fell on me. 'What's wrong, hinny?'

Tom Verger peered down at me, brow crinkled in concern. The man my mother had betrayed my father with. It was unbearable, knowing that the people I thought of as my family were only kind strangers who'd taken me in and lied to me.

'What's all this, Rose? What's going on? Has someone hurt you?'

Tom Verger was the last person I wanted to talk to but also the best person if I wanted the truth. He held out his hand so I took it, stood up and followed him into his shack, Barebones beside me. He closed the door softly behind us, sat me on a cracket near the fire and gave me his kerchief. I wiped away my tears with the rough cheesecloth, glad to have something to hide behind. It was strange being in this hut. Of course, I'd been in it as a child because Reverend Foster often fetched me in and I'd sit on his knee and listen to him talking to Tom and Bill Verger. They were all good men. But it was awkward sitting with this man now, knowing he might be my natural father.

'Tell me what's put you in this state, Rose. It won't go any further than me, if that's how you want it.'

I shared everything, and as my words reached him, his grave expression told me Patience Leaton was telling the truth. But I had to hear it from him.

'Are you my father?'

'Ah, Rose, I'd hoped you'd be older and more settled in life afore this all came out. But aye, it is true. How did you find out? That busybody at the manse?'

I nodded.

'Naught better to do all day than poke her nose into other people's concerns.'

'Everyone knows about me except for me. Please, Mr Verger, the vicar's daughter used terrible words about my mother and I need to know. Will you please tell me?'

'First, call me Tom. Can you do that, do you think?'

I nodded, relieved he hadn't asked me to call him Da.

'Your mother was a good woman, Rose, and if the vicar's daughter says otherwise, then she's a liar.'

And so he held my hands and told me that he, Tom Verger, was my real father, and that he'd loved my mother. I'd been conceived a month ahead of the day they were due to marry, but Tom had been press-ganged into naval service, so the wedding hadn't gone ahead. Da had connived to marry my mother, tricking her into believing Tom dead after being reported lost at sea. This behaviour sounded like Da, but I'd not take another man's word for it when he couldn't defend himself.

'Except you're not lost at sea, are you?' I said.

'Aye, God spared me. But when I came home, I found

your mother married to your Da. It was a terrible time. The both of us knocking lumps out of each other. Me as bad as him, I'm sorry to say. With your little brother on his way, the bishop wouldn't release your mother from the marriage. So, all these years, I've loved you but stood back for your sake. When your mother and brother passed, it would have been cruel to take you away from the people you thought of as your family so soon after. You needed a steady home. Those were dark days, Rose. Dark days.'

I hated Patience Leaton for her spite but also the Drivers and the Vergers and Reverend Foster and even the mart wives for keeping this from me. Everyone knew this secret, it seemed. Everyone but me. Da must have silenced them all. Now I was all alone and no longer a Driver but a Verger. No matter how hard I tried, there were no memories of my mother in my head, and all I knew of her came from other people's descriptions. I couldn't even feel sad at her passing, because some kind of big, grey mass in my head stopped me feeling anything when they spoke of her.

It was stupid of me to run so near to the manse, but I needed some answers. Now I had them, I'd run far away or the Leatons would force me to marry and have this child. There was no chance of me surviving childbed when it only led to death and sorrow for the women in my family. My mother, Grandmother Verger and Earnest's mother had not survived childbed. So many dead women.

Wedlock

PATIENCE

My brother was to be married at daybreak, to the by-blow of a gravedigger. First though, we had to catch his bride, who absconded immediately on learning she would be kept under guard. Due to her lack of forethought, we soon found her in the gravedigger's hut. My father would not countenance the prospective bride jilting my brother and destroying his name. After forcibly returning her to the farmstead, there she was kept under close watch by me and Green, who had turned her coat very much in our favour.

The bed was too narrow for three and Driver spent her last two nights as a spinster taking up all the space in the middle, whilst we clung to the sides. As a result, none of us slept and we were all paler than milk come the morning of the wedding.

As we walked uphill, the bell sounded across the valley. The same bell rang for weddings as for funerals and a skilled sexton could make it toll or peal accordingly. Today, the bell tolled.

Following the revelation of Rose Driver's paternity, we had still not aired her family's unwillingness to observe the sabbath, and I cursed myself for not addressing that before revealing her bastardy.

Father was so determined to spare his son's good name that he compromised on all aspects of the nuptials. Because of the Drivers' reluctance to cross the church threshold, the ceremony would be held outdoors. Father intended to remain in the vestry doorway so he at least stood in the church. All most irregular but he assured us that the marriage would be valid and the child legitimate.

Green and I followed Rose Driver up the hill. She was flanked by her stepmother and grandmother, with her dog loping at heel. Despite exhortations from her grandmother, the bride refused to make any concession and wore her usual undyed wool frock, left her mane uncovered, and in place of a posy, carried her crook as if it were a cudgel. For his part, Earnest faced the vestry door, buttoned up in his best clothes, face stiff and shuttered beneath his tall hat, never once turning to look at his intended.

Despite the early hour, the service was well attended by the Driver widows both, Thomas Verger, big Blenkinsop and the Greens, including Matilda, who was permitted to take the morning off instead of next Sunday afternoon as a boon. Should the bride discover who had sold her secrets to me, she might not be so keen to welcome her former bedmate as a witness.

When the tolling bell ceased, Elizabeth Driver's eye fell on her family grave and I feared an emotional outburst but she contented herself with a loud sniff and a complaint that there was barely anyone in attendance.

Father and the elderly widow were agreed on one aspect. To avoid undue upset, Thomas Verger would be allowed no formal role in the ceremony. Instead, Farmer Johnson would give away the bride. He collected his ward from the lych gate and escorted her to the vestry door, and we fell in behind. As we proceeded through the churchyard, Johnson raised his chin in greeting to Verger, who had finished bell-ringing and strolled towards the vestry.

Father accepted his presence with remarkable

equanimity because he needed this marriage to proceed as much as Earnest did, and the last thing he wanted was the sexton objecting.

For the occasion, Thomas Verger had put on his Sunday coat, which strained at the shoulders. As dawn broke, the sun lit his hair in gold and my eyes were drawn to him. Perhaps like Mother, badness lurked within, making me yearn for a fellow guilty of bastardy.

Yet again, our sexton had plucked some blowsy white roses from the sprawl growing up the manse. One, he sported in his buttonhole and the remainder he had tied with twine. The audacity of the man! As Thomas Verger passed, Farmer Johnson pressed a hand to his shoulder and in turn, Verger pressed the stolen posy into his daughter's free hand. It would be a lie to say I wasn't touched by the exquisite pain Verger must be feeling, watching his daughter on another man's arm. Even so, it did not excuse theft, so I confiscated both the posy and the buttonhole and defied anyone to say a word.

Accompanied by her ever-present collie, the bride knelt at the wooden crosses that commemorated her mother, her brother, and both of her grandmothers. Tears welled in her eyes as she kissed her fingers and touched them to each marker.

Judging by the number of the bride's female relatives resting in the churchyard, her chances of surviving childbed were low, and no doubt we would be encumbered with any surviving infant. Still, a lot could happen between now and then. We waited whilst she and her womenfolk proceeded to the Drivers' plot to repeat the sentimental ritual.

When the bride straightened up, Father prodded the reluctant groom in the chest and nodded at his hat, so he removed it. After some gesticulation by her grandmother, the bride handed over her crook. My brother took his future goodwife's hand, and the sparse congregation closed around them. Father held out his open Bible and Earnest placed my grandmother's gold ring on the pages. Father waited until he had his congregation's attention.

'Everyone, before we begin, do not worry that we are standing outside. This land is sanctified and we are all in God's sight.'

'Mebbes someone should've mentioned that to the bishop and saved the parish a fortune in dressed stone,' muttered Blenkinsop, receiving a sharp glance from me for his blasphemous outburst.

Mercifully, the masquerade would be over soon, and due to its proximity to a recent bereavement, there would be no wedding breakfast afterwards. The abbreviated service involved scarcely more than the exchange of espousal vows as Father dispensed with his usual sermon. Since hymns were frowned upon, there was no singing, but as the air warmed, the dawn chorus began.

Rose Driver shuddered as my brother slid our grandmother's ring onto her finger. A sure indication that she could not stand to be touched by any holy artefact. With a shove from Farmer Johnson, Earnest enveloped her in his arms. An endeavour as unnecessary as it was unwanted when everyone present knew that the bride had already been kissed, and more.

Rosemary for Remembrance

ROSE

The wedding was quick with no breakfast afterwards. Apart from showing respect to Da, with so much work to do, Granny wanted me back home as soon as it was over, but Minister Leaton had other ideas.

'Earnest,' he said, 'do not forget to bring your bride.'

No one had mentioned any need to live at the manse. I had to resist or I'd be finished. Granny would refuse to let me go, if only to keep me working the farm because May couldn't manage it on her own.

'There's no need for me to do their bidding, Granny, or to move in with them. I'm married to Earnest fair and square and have his name so it barely matters where I live.'

'It matters a great deal,' said Minister Leaton. 'You are a Leaton now and you will live in our home.'

'What's this?' asked Granny. 'Why can't Rosie stay put with me and May? After all, your lad's putting to sea in a matter of days and we could use the help, at least till he gets back...'

If he gets back, she meant.

Minister Leaton looked set to waver, but his daughter whispered in his ear and he nodded at her.

'Since this woman is not your true granddaughter, I

cannot trust that you will value her or my grandchild enough to protect them so she must live with us. The future of the farm is not my concern, but the future of my grandchild certainly is. You can keep the dog, of course, since I refuse to give it houseroom.'

The fight had gone out of Granny so I tried, without success, to catch May's eye. She must realise I didn't want this child and would smuggle a remedy to me.

Barebones came to me and I knelt and rubbed her breast where she liked it best. She thumped her tail but her eyes were sorrowful. Though it pained me, I ordered her to stay and turned away from her, my chin quivering as I determined not to cry or turn around when she whimpered. Granny passed my crook to me but Earnest intercepted it and handed it back to her.

'My goodwife will have no further need for that, Widow Driver, since her days of roaming outdoors are behind her.'

So I'd lost my family, my dog, my flock and my home, as well as the sky and the dale. And soon I would lose my life.

The Leaton men each seized an arm, and with Patience to the fore and Tilly aft, the five of us walked towards my new home, silent and in close formation. When we reached the manse, my captors released my arms and I rubbed them to bring back the feeling. Minister Leaton locked the door behind us and pocketed the key. He followed Patience and Tilly upstairs, leaving Earnest at their foot to bar me from going up after them.

My new husband was a stranger to me and not the same man I'd allowed to kiss and caress me out of my senses. Foolish to a fault, I'd believed him in love with me, a man I'd known for a season. All my resolutions had fallen aside. For the sake of a few minutes of pleasure, I'd sacrificed my whole future.

Instead of years ahead of me, walking the hills and tending to my flock, sitting by the warm fire of an evening, spinning yarns with Granny and May and petting

Barebones, I'd soon be dead, and my child with me. Even supposing we lived, what would be the point among these cold and loveless people?

I eyed the staircase stretching up to the first landing. It was long and steep and would end my misery if I could summon the courage.

'Be my guest, Rose,' said Earnest, a cruel smile playing on his lips. 'I won't stand in your way and would go to sea with a lighter heart.'

He took a step to the left and I dashed past him to the top of the stairs. Panting, I caught my breath, unable to believe I'd been reduced to this. Earnest looked up at me, waving his arm with a small flourish. I pulled my hand away from the banister and lifted a foot from the stair, but my gorge rose as I leant into the void, and I grabbed at the handrail, my heart racing.

Earnest scoffed. 'Can't bring yourself to do the dark deed? Shall I come up there and do it for you?'

I was terrified of having this baby but more so of falling down the stairs. My mind encouraged me to do it, but my body prevented me. Humiliated, I walked back down. May coming to my rescue was my only hope.

While I waited to see what was in store for me, I went wandering in my mother's childhood home. How would she judge me, knowing what I planned to do? Dying the way she had, I felt sure she wouldn't want the same to happen to me, and were she still alive, she'd help me to restore my courses.

It gave me some comfort to think of her living here, working alongside Grandmother Chandler, and I entered each room, trying to remember anything from the time before tragedy struck my family.

I found the old pantry, where the sun shone, making it warm and bright. On the ceiling was a drying rack. I untied the rope securing it, let it down to waist-height and thought of my mother and grandmother tying bunches of herbs to it in this sunny room. Perhaps sage or mint or rosemary.

Rosemary for remembrance, the mart wives claimed, but it had never helped me.

I strived to remember my mother and her mother, perhaps with me sitting on the high bench and them laughing together or singing to me while they worked. But there it was again, that mass of grey, sealing my memories from me so there was naught of either woman except what the mart wives had told me, and that was not something to dwell on.

My throat clogged with tears at the thought of the brave women who'd been taken from me. They would have helped me. They wouldn't let me sacrifice myself for a child that would more than likely kill me.

Here in this room, breathing in the essence of them, I felt calmer. Might there be some slight chance of not dying in childbed and living long enough to raise my child? Only nine moons lay between today and my due date. My life had been so short and I wasn't done with it. Yet, this child in my belly hadn't lived at all, and what right had I to cling to life at his expense? The thought fetched a heavy sigh from me.

'I don't know what you're sighing about,' said Patience Leaton from the door. 'Your husband is leaving for his ship and you must say goodbye, for who knows when you two will meet again.'

I had no interest in saying goodbye to Earnest, but Patience called Tilly into the pantry and together they escorted me to the front door. He stood just outside, a valise at his feet.

'My father and sister will care for you while I am gone, goodwife. Try not to displease them.'

I stood apart while he embraced his sister and clasped his father's hand then lifted the valise and walked down the valley to where Farmer Johnson waited with his wagon. I did not watch as they set off along the low road to Newcastle.

A Good Puritan Woman

PATIENCE

I considered my sister-in-law in her new garb. I had confiscated the light woollen robe that did nothing to disguise her condition and burnt it on the kitchen fire. She was now clad in a worsted murrey garment that smelt musty but was otherwise sound and her fiery hair was bound in a coif. The dress was at half-mast and stretched across her belly. Its sleeves were too short and pulled at her wrists, hemming her in. The addition of a collar and apron helped to disguise her protruding breasts and belly. Imprisonment in her new clothes would curtail her movements so she would be more sedate and Leaton-like.

The overall effect was of a strait-laced and sober young matron. I had erased the heathen shepherdess to make way for a good puritan woman. All that remained of Rose Driver was the green of her eyes and the red of her lips. Were it possible to subdue those, I would do it. How vital she had appeared the day I first met her and how drab she was today. The man she thought of as her father was dead, the people she thought of as her family were no more than strangers, her belly was full of an unwanted child and she was at my mercy.

'This dress belonged to my mother,' I said. 'She wore it

while carrying twins, so it should do you, although I doubt you are worthy of it.'

'It belonged to your mother, who died in childbed?'

I only just prevented myself from correcting her. An unguarded moment and a timely reminder to watch my step. This woman must never learn that my mother was almost certainly still alive and living in sin somewhere with Father's former curate. I would speak to Green about spending her afternoons off gossiping about her employers.

'Yes, my mother who died in childbed. God rest her.'

On hearing this, my sister-in-law grasped a handful of the heavy fabric as if to tear it from her body. It was a lot of fuss over a frock.

'Where are Mother's shoes?' I asked.

'They don't fit me.'

'We shall soon see about that.'

But even I could see that her ungainly farmer's feet would not fit into my mother's dainty shoes. Whilst reluctant to concede defeat, I permitted her to continue wearing her old boots.

'I suppose it will not matter, considering where you are headed.'

She scowled and I ushered her upstairs, along the landing, past our chambers and up a twisting staircase that ended at a locked door. There, I took the key from my apron pocket and opened it.

'Where are you taking me?'

'To your new quarters. My father feels it better you should be left in peace until this child is born.'

My prisoner paused. Beyond us lay the garret, with its narrow passage and solitary attic room where Green had lodged hitherto. Father wanted to quarter the mother of his grandchild up here for her own safety and to prevent her from throwing herself down the stairs or over the banister. Ever the slattern, Green had made no effort to clean or brighten her former accommodation so cobwebs trailed from the ceiling and fireplace alike. Father would be displeased if he saw them, so Green would have to come in and dust around my sister-in-law. The grate over the Bible-sized window meant it could not be opened, leaving the room hot and unaired. The long curtains had been removed and the room was empty, apart from a straw mattress, a bolster and a copper chamber pot.

'Our servant will fetch your meals and change your pot. You are free to wander the top storey.' No need to labour the point that there was no exit except through the locked door.

'I'm to stay up here, away from everyone I love, with nobody to talk to? Granny needs me to help with the harvest and the livestock and she'll not cope without me.'

She ran to the window and pushed her face against the grate. There would be no fresh air, but she could enjoy a patch of sky, and beneath the canopy of leafy trees, she could see part of the churchyard and the church itself. Whilst she was occupied, I withdrew, walked along the passage, closed the door behind me and turned the key.

Instantly, I heard her running along the passage towards the door, battering on it with her fists.

'There's no air, and I'll suffocate in this heat. You can't keep me up here at the height of summer.'

'I dare say that we can.'

'Granny won't stand for this. Making me live with my husband's family is one thing, but keeping me captive is quite another. I'll ask Tilly to get a message to Granny.'

'May you meet with success.' I smiled and patted the key in my pocket. Green knew which side her bread was buttered and my sister-in-law would not be going anywhere, anytime soon. At least, not until I had amassed sufficient proof to secure a conviction against her, having learnt the necessity of this from prior experience.

Despite my efforts, the Ely witch had evaded justice when the indifferent authorities released her. Our old housekeeper should have hanged but the evidence against her was judged insufficiently damning to bring her to trial. Cook told me that on hearing of the housekeeper's arrest, my father had hurried straight to the gaol to swear the woman was of good character and cautioned the authorities to take more care about whose accusations they believed. Betrayed by my own father! His efforts were to no avail though, because our housekeeper's short incarceration so withered her that she perished from gaol fever after a few weeks of freedom. Although she died anyway, a natural death was not punishment enough in my considered opinion.

The housekeeper's arrest and its aftermath had not sat well with Father. Upon learning of her death, he prayed for her soul and that of her child. Even though the child was not fully formed, he secretly baptised the corpse and buried it with its mother inside the churchyard, paying the gravedigger from his own purse and blessing the grave.

Our former housekeeper had escaped her rightful punishment because of my juvenile impetuosity and my father's lack of faith in me. I would not make the same mistake twice.

AUTUMN

A Dark Vial

The only way of telling how many weeks I'd been imprisoned was by counting Sundays when most of the parish went to church. People came and went, and a few times, I'd seen Granny and May approach the door, and sometimes Tom Verger, only to be turned away. I called down but they were so far below, they never heard me and I wondered how the Leatons fobbed them off. Often, Barebones would turn up and sit in the graveyard, gazing skywards. My heart swelled when I saw her barking silently. My good lass was the only member of my family who knew I was in trouble. Tilly had sided with the Leatons and wouldn't say a word to May so I doubted my family realised I was trapped up here, and even if they did, what could they do anyway?

Every morning, I vomited on waking and the pall of nausea hung over me till evening. May had let me down and I'd not heard a word from her. Judging by the size of my belly, it would soon be too late, and I'd have to bear this child. There were no sharp implements or anything with an edge and I had to eat my meals with a short spoon that was always removed from me. My bed was just a soft pallet on the floor. Along with my meals, I received an empty metal pot draped with a cloth. My captors wouldn't allow me porcelain for fear I smash it to injure myself. My window was grated and impossible to open, and in any case too narrow for me to climb through, but at least I could see trees and birds and people.

I watched Tom Verger and tried to get used to the idea of him as my father. Summer had just turned into autumn, and the weather was still mild so there weren't many deaths, and he spent his days sharpening tools, tending graves and sweeping up the orange and gold leaves that were starting to fall from the trees.

The mound over Da's grave hadn't yet settled and I struggled to accept he was under there. Somewhere in my head, I convinced myself that he was alive and at the fair on the Town Moor. If he were still alive, I could be angry at him for his treatment of my mother and May but it was hard to hate a dead man.

Tom Verger sometimes looked over at the manse but never raised his eyes to the attic and why should he? Who would expect me to be trapped up here? It was strange, watching this man. We shared the same blood but I didn't know him and probably never would. Had he really left me with the Drivers as a kindness to me or to suit himself because he'd lost my mother and had no further interest in me? Da was far from perfect, but at least he'd taken on the unwanted cade lamb.

❧

Tilly came into my room, carrying my mother's old leather satchel and my heart lifted at the sight of it. May must have called at the manse. She'd not forgotten me after all. I faced away from Tilly so she wouldn't see what was in my eyes.

'Your belongings. Our May fetched them up ages ago.

Patience hung on to them till she had time to check through the bag and said you could keep them once she saw it was just swaddling bands and so on. Mind, she wasn't best pleased about your old red stockings.'

I opened the satchel. Inside were miniature woollen frocks, vests and mittens, and I took out each item and held it up. Some were knitted for me and others for my brother, who'd not lived long enough to wear them. Granny had shown these to me when I was a bairn and even then I could see how precious they were to her. She must be heartbroken parting with such treasure, so I'd look after them. It wasn't lost on me that I'd take better care of these tiny garments than the tiny person they were intended to clothe. My scarlet stockings were there and so impossibly small it was a marvel my feet had ever fitted into them.

'You want to consider yourself lucky I never got round to hoying those on the fire like madam told me to.'

Tilly was as cold towards me as Patience lately, but she said this kindly and it felt almost as though we were old friends again. When I unfolded my christening shawl, something fell out. She picked it up and passed it to me.

'Gyb! Fancy your granny keeping that for all these years. You wouldn't be parted from it when you were a bairn.'

So that's where it had gone. I'd mislaid it once and bawled my eyes out for days. Granny and Granda had turned the farmstead upside down looking for it. I'd keep it safe now, inside my bodice and away from Patience Leaton and her fires. I ran my finger over the small wooden cat.

'Bill Verger made it for me. It was my present for being the Candlemas maid. Some old tradition, Da reckoned.'

Tilly sniffed. 'Well, Bill Verger never gave me a present when I was the maid the year before you. Still, as it turns out, he was your grandfather, so that's mebbes why he favoured you. You wore those red stockings that Candlemas. Do you remember?'

Unbidden, the memory rose of me cavorting in them before the manse window, admiring the candle crown in my hair and crying when the pretty flames went out, begging my unseen mother to make them return. That was the last night my mother was alive. I held the stockings to my face, breathing in the wool, knowing this wasn't my own memory but one borrowed from Granny.

&.

In the early hours, my mouth was wet with the saliva that meant being sick. Afterwards, I thought about the satchel. May would never let me down and she'd certainly not be so cruel as to send a pile of baby clothes and naught else. I emptied out the satchel again, forced my fingernails down either side of the base and prised it free. Beneath was an indentation, filled with tufts of wool. After teasing them out, I found nested in them a flattish circular bottle with a stopper. It fitted in the palm of my hand, its dark liquid absorbing the weak sunlight. May hadn't forgotten me.

The grey clouds moved slowly in the sky and I watched them, wondering whether I could do this to myself, to the child who was not yet a child. Below, Tom Verger's hut was just a dark outline and I thought of the crosses next to it. My mother and brother, who'd died on the day of his birth. And Tom Verger's mother who'd died on the day of his birth. It was cowardly to put myself before an innocent child, but I didn't want to leave this life, and even if I somehow survived, I didn't want to spend that life with Earnest Leaton. Without thinking any further, I unstopped the vial and swallowed the bitter remedy, gagging at the taste and smell, and panting in an attempt to keep the awful julep down because there wouldn't be another chance.

It would be unwise to replace the vial and wool tufts in the satchel. Patience had searched it, but not too thoroughly. Once the remedy did its work, she might search it again, and if she discovered the vial, it could cost me my neck and May hers, so I crossed to the fireplace and pushed my arm up the chimney, feeling about for a ledge. There was a small crevice and I wedged the glass bottle into it. Providing Tilly didn't sweep too thoroughly, it should stay safely hidden.

The Nightwalker

PATIENCE

The sound of feet pattering up and down the passage overhead woke me. What was that accursed woman up to? I rang for Green to rise so she could put my sister-in-law back to bed but our servant slept like a hibernating beast. It would take longer to rouse her than to see to the nightwalker myself so I lit a candle and pulled on my robe. The manse was colder than the crypt at night, even at the height of what passed for summer in Mutton Clog, and as it was now autumn, I shivered on my way along the landing.

The loss of my sister-in-law's child would be of no concern to me, but Father wanted the child alive, sacrificing my brother's future happiness in the attempt. I crept up the quarter stair, unlocked the door, and there she was in full flight, damp white nightdress clinging to her, arms outstretched, mouth open in a silent scream. In the flickering candlelight, her gigantic shadow chased her and I trembled at the uncanny sight. Her eyes were wide open, yet unseeing and she hurtled towards me. If she tripped and landed on her belly, she would hurt the child, and Father would never believe me not responsible, so she would have to go safely back to bed. I flattened myself against the wall and once she passed me, I entered her chamber, hoping that the light from my flame might somehow catch her eye and draw her inwards, moth-like.

It worked and she paused at the door, looking yet not seeing, as if lost. I guided her into bed and stared at her belly, visible through her damp nightdress, unable to resist touching it. Beneath my hand, her hot flesh moved. It repulsed me, knowing my brother's child moved within her, perhaps disturbed by the nightwalker. The quickening! So this child now had a soul.

&.

On my second rising, the sky remained grey, but by the time I was dressed and downstairs, the curtains were open to reveal a sky tinged with red. Shepherd's warning, according to the superstitious folk in the quarter. Without having to be asked, Green fetched me some warm milk and bread, and she stoked the fire.

'Madam,' she said, 'You look awful tired this morning.'

'Thank you for telling me what I already know.'

'Sorry, madam. No harm meant. Just concerned for your health.'

'My health is not under question.' I wiped some dripping onto a pinch of bread and took a bite. 'That unnatural woman was up in the night, roaming the landing in her sleep, yet you neglected to wake and do your duty.'

The servant continued busying herself with the fire and failed to reply, but I was too tired to upbraid the girl either for her idleness or her lack of manners.

'Green,' I said at length, 'when you shared a room with Goodwife Leaton, did she often rise in the night?'

'No, madam, I cannot say she did,' said the girl. 'But she used to have nightmares as a child. That's why the Drivers were keen to have me share her bed so I could comfort her. It used to scare me senseless. Our May tried all sorts of tisanes. Chamomile. Lavender. Valerian.'

I could hardly breathe. This sinister behaviour was a frank admission of witchcraft in the Driver household.

'And were your sister's potions effective?'

Green stopped working and stood up. Any chance to idle and the indolent girl would take it, but I would let her dawdle all she liked in return for information.

'Oh, aye. For a while, at least. She went years without any bad dreams, but when her courses came, it set her off again. Then as she got older, she settled down, or at least seemed to till this latest spell.'

Green knew more than she was letting on. She had foxed me the last time, taking the looking glass and brush and fobbing me off with inferior gossip. I had no more pretty possessions to bribe her with as the sandglasses did not appeal to her vanity. Without any more appealing trinkets to offer, some cunning would be necessary.

'Come, sit by me and take a bite to eat.'

Pert as ever, Green turned up her nose at the bread and dripping. Evidently, her ladyship had dined on better fodder with the Drivers. Since I had overseen her letting out the seams and forbidden her from adjusting her garments again, her frock now hung loose from her newly lean frame.

'Tell me, do you know what caused these nightmares?'

Green shook her head slowly. 'No one knows. Rosie – Goodwife Leaton – could never remember anything on waking.'

I would wager that someone did know, but they were not telling. It occurred to me that my sister-in-law was unhappy in the garret, but otherwise calm, until Green took her the old leather satchel.

'The night you delivered the swaddling clothes to the attic, that was only hours before the start of Goodwife Leaton's nightwalking. Does that not strike you as a suspicious coincidence?'

The girl flushed, guilty with knowledge. It simply remained for me to draw it from her.

'Green, I am very fond of you, as is my father.' This had the desired effect, and she raised her eyes to me. 'As a widower, he has been alone for a long time, ever since my mother died, may God have mercy on her soul. I suppose one day I might marry and leave, and he will be all alone...'

I took her left hand between both of mine and coaxed her into the chair beside me, allowing the notion of marriage to hang in the air. Apparently, Green had been given reason to entertain hopes for my brother, but these had been dashed at the mill pond. Marriage to my father could never be permitted to happen, not whilst my wicked mother still walked the earth, and of course I could not tolerate a servant as my stepmother, but Green remained ignorant of these facts.

'Father has asked me several times recently about a newly widowed woman, the wife of a former acquaintance of his. She is highly suitable, of course, and most fair.'

Green rubbed at her brow with her free hand and I sensed she would prefer to withdraw her other hand from mine, but I kept it nursed between my own and would not let go until she spilt all her secrets.

'Andrew Driver made us all swear never to mention a word of this,' she said, gnawing her bottom lip, 'and my only reason for telling you now is because I fear for Goodwife Leaton, you understand.'

I took her free hand so both her hands were trapped between mine. 'You do right to fear for her, Matilda. We all do. And we all want the same. To care for Goodwife Leaton. My father will learn of your role in helping her, you may be sure of that. Perhaps you should start by fetching the satchel to me. Go quietly. It will be better if my sister-in-law remains asleep.'

❧

Green returned with the satchel, her head down, and despite the lure of marriage to my father, it had clearly cost her something to fetch it to me. She placed it on the table and opened it out to reveal a great many infant-sized woollens, which she lifted out and stacked in neat piles. I picked up a small vest and tried to imagine my brother's child wearing it. So small and admittedly rather sweet, even though no urge for motherhood had ever troubled me. Green held up some scarlet stockings and smiled to herself, sharing my sentiment.

'No child in this house will be seen wearing such garish attire. Did I not instruct you to burn those?'

She nodded, hugging them to her. There was no time to address her insurrection so I would deal with her and the gaudy stockings later. Once the satchel was completely empty, I examined it again but more thoroughly this time. Looking at the satchel side on, it became apparent to me that the inner base stood two or three inches proud of its studded bottom. At my instruction, Green fetched a pair of butter knives and pushed the blunt blades down either side of the base. As suspected, it came away and she lifted it out, revealing a hidden compartment that could have stored contraband.

'Your sister fetched this satchel, Green. Would you put it past her to help kill a child?'

I could have bitten my lips off for blundering in with such a blunt question because the girl held her hands up to her mouth, eyes wide. She was torn between protecting her sister and furthering herself. Gently, I took hold of her fingers and prised them free.

'Green, listen. My father will take it badly if my brother's child is murdered, and it will be murder because the quickening has taken place. I felt it just hours ago with my own hand. The child now has a soul. Help me, and I can protect you and your sister. If you refuse to assist, then I cannot guarantee what will happen to either of you.'

'I want to help you, madam. Truly, I do. But the Drivers were so kind to me.'

Green's misplaced loyalty irritated me, but she must not sense my impatience or she would hold her tongue. Whilst a young woman ridding herself of an unwanted child was not necessarily a sign of unholy power, once the quickening had taken place, it must be a crime in both the eyes of God and in the eyes of the law.

Green's eyes slid sidewards. Whatever she hoped to gain from me and my father, she still bore some vestige of kinship to her old bedmate and to her sister. It was most exasperating. If Green betrayed her family, she would do it in her own sweet time, no doubt enjoying herself at my expense, knowing I had no choice but to rely on her.

'It's better if I show you, madam.'

I followed her upstairs to the attic room where my sister-in-law slept, opened the door and crept into her chamber. Green tiptoed to the newly dusted fireplace, knelt down inside the unlit ingle and reached up the chimney. When she pulled out her hand, it held a ball of wool scraps, which she offered to me. I refused to touch them, so she unravelled them herself. In their midst lay an empty glass bottle, with a stopper in it. An involuntary shiver ran up my spine.

'Remove the stopper, Green,' I whispered, conscious that its owner might wake. Cautiously, she did my bidding. 'Now hold it up to my nose.'

I inhaled a trace of mint, along with a resinous scent that cleared my head so quickly it left me faint.

Poison! What conjuration had taken place? I imagined my sister-in-law drinking from the bottle and muttering some sickening incantation.

'This is nothing short of devilry,' I said. 'Green, tell me the truth. Is your sister a witch?'

Green recoiled at the accusation. 'No, no. I promise you, she's just a farmer's wife – widow.' She scrubbed at her eyes. 'Our May's not a witch, I swear, not like Goodwife Leaton.'

'O, so Goodwife Leaton is a witch?'

Green gnawed her lip so hard she almost drew blood. I must not startle her for she was on the brink of telling me something incriminating and a new tack was necessary.

'Fear not, Matilda,' I murmured. 'I bear no grudge against your sister. Whatever you share with me, I promise before God it will not hurt her.'

'Do you swear, madam?'

I placed my hand over my heart. 'Your sister will come to no harm.'

She swallowed and closed her eyes for a moment, then nodded, and I knew she was my creature now.

'Tell me,' I said, 'why the Drivers do not go to church. Do not fear the truth, for you are on the side of God, and He will protect you in return for doing His work.'

Green was glassy-eyed, drunk with her forbidden tale. She allowed herself a last glance at my sleeping sister-in-law before she told me what I needed to know. My instinct in employing her had paid off more handsomely than I could have dared to hope.

A woman called Annie Chandler had been the Reverend Foster's hearth woman as well as the local midwife, with her daughter Jane as apprentice. Both women had been accused of witchcraft in Newcastle some twenty years ago. Annie was hanged but Jane escaped justice, thanks to an intervention by Foster. And Jane's daughter was none other than Rose Driver! I had suspected her of witchcraft when I caught her at her bloody rite with the lamb, but never had I dreamt of uncovering evidence as damning as this.

'So, my sister-in-law is descended from a proven witch and an accused witch?'

'Aye,' whispered Green. 'That's why she cannot set foot in church.'

How had this momentous news escaped me? But before

I could question our servant further, a furious voice interrupted us.

'How can you be so cruel, Tilly Green? And after all my family's done for you. My Grandmother Chandler was never a witch and neither was my mother.'

Green held her ground admirably. 'I'm not telling lies. Annie Chandler *was* hanged as a witch. You were just a bairn, and me not much older, but I remember it all. Your ma was due to be next at the gallows but Reverend Foster spared her.'

'They were only innocent midwives, Tilly, and you know it!'

Our servant had the temerity to slip behind me to shield herself from my sister-in-law, who was stalking towards us. She reached beyond me and plucked the vial from Green's hand. Her glittering green eyes were terrifying but her finger shook as she pointed at us and her voice held a tremor, despite its volume.

'You'd better keep away from me Tilly Green! I can't believe you were ever my friend, and as for you, Patience Leaton, you've no business going through my belongings.'

Her shouting must have roused my father, who now stood in the doorway, silver hair standing in peaks, face softened by sleep. He looked so young it was almost as if my brother were standing at the door instead.

'I suppose the church must be on fire for you all to be up and about and making such a racket at this hour.' He marched to the window and peered out. 'Yet I see no flames. Neither do I smell any smoke. So what is it, Patience? What is going on here?'

'May I speak to you privately, Father?'

'You may not. Spit it out, whatever it is, or I am going back to bed.'

I ignored the pleading eyes of both Green and my sister-in-law and turned to answer my father.

'Beneath our noses, Goodwife Leaton has procured a

bottle of poison, and I believe she has taken it with the intention of killing her unborn child. Furthermore, her maternal grandmother was a known witch, executed for consorting with the devil. Her own mother was accused alongside her and was only spared by the intervention of your predecessor. This proves, does it not, that we are most likely sheltering a witch? God alone knows what she has bred in her belly, but I suspect it is not my brother's child. Now that the foetus has quickened, she needs to kill the child to release its corrupted soul – who knows for what end?'

My father's grave expression told me that my words had made their mark. He no longer doubted me and this would make my plan all the easier to execute. But first, we would have to go to church and cleanse our own souls.

The Shortening of the Days
ROSE

All night, bad dreams plagued me and I woke up as exhausted as if I'd never slept. A pink sky lit up the window but I saw no benefit in getting up now I was confined to my chamber, having lost the small freedom of the passage. Instead, I was reduced to pacing the confines of my room, with little to break the monotony beyond looking through the grated window at the trees shedding their brown leaves in the graveyard.

Ever since the Leatons found the empty vial, they'd kept me under even closer watch, with Tilly as keen a guard as Patience. May's remedy hadn't worked beyond creating a dull ache in the pit of my belly, and naught had come away. This baby would be born and its birth would be as good as a death sentence for me.

I understood why Tilly had sided with the Leatons – she wanted to keep her job – but I'd never forgive my former friend for slandering Grandmother Chandler and my mother. It was terrible hearing those words coming out of her mouth.

❧

The morning turned drizzly, which suited my mood, and I leant against the wall, watching out of the window, when the sight of a horse stirred me. The rider tied it up at the lych gate and made his way through the graveyard with great haste. A short time later, he left the way he'd come, mounted his horse and rode off.

By late afternoon, I'd been locked in my room all day. Nobody had come near me, not even Tilly with a tray of food, and my chamber pot stank. Whatever the message fetched by the horseman, it had interrupted the manse's strict routines. I was hungry and thirsty and sickened by the stench of my own waste. The Leatons were unkind but never did I expect them to deprive me like this. It must be something to do with the horseman, but what?

I put my eye to the grated window. Below me, through the trees, Tom Verger crouched over a wooden cross. If I had a stick, I could poke it through the grate to shatter the glass and attract his attention, but there were no sticks and calling out was useless when the attic was so high up. I was entirely at the mercy of my keepers. Minister Leaton was angry the night of the vial and had confined me to my room but he'd never withheld food or drink, and Tilly changed my pot every day without fail. It made no sense for him to punish me this way when he wanted my child to survive.

Night fell and still no one had come to see me. Just as I was beginning to fear that no one would come again, I heard footsteps on the quarter stair and the door being unlocked. Hopefully, it was Tilly with at least a flask of water, but the approaching footsteps suggested Tilly together with Patience.

Tilly entered first, head down. She scurried to the corner, picked up my chamber pot and left without raising her eyes or saying a word. Patience then entered, holding a pricket in one hand and a piece of paper in the other. She was even more wan than usual and her eyes were bloodshot.

'You have a right to see this, I suppose.' She thrust the paper at me.

I made no move to take it from her and kept my hands at my sides.

'You know I cannot read, Patience, so you'll have to tell me what it says.'

'This paper contains the news that Earnest has been killed.' She held it out to me again and I took it from her. 'Look at it. My brother has fallen in active duty. The fleet faltered in its advance on the Dutch and his vessel was overwhelmed. My brother was lost and many men besides.'

This news seemed unlikely, not least because Earnest had gone to sea only a matter of weeks ago. Hadn't he? Time passed increasingly slowly of late, and if not for the shortening of the days and the increasing size of my belly, I'd believe it had stopped altogether.

'Earnest is only presumed lost at sea,' I said, keen to get on Patience's right side. 'Tom Verger was the same, presumed dead, but he returned. The same might yet happen with Earnest—'

She slapped me, and my face stung from her hard little hand. I swallowed and touched my fingers to my face.

'Do not raise false hopes. My brother is dead and so are the men on his ship.' Tears blurted from her eyes. 'Earnest's body is broken and he will lie forever at the bottom of a cold sea off a foreign shore. Alone, now and forever.'

It shocked me to see Patience weeping. She'd really loved her brother, and no matter how unkind he was, I'd wish no man such a terrible death.

'I'll forgive you that blow, Patience, because you're in mourning for your brother. But you will never strike me again. I'm your brother's widow, after all.'

'My brother's widow.' She laughed strangely, her voice cracking. 'You are a low-born witch, descended from a long line of low-born witches and gravediggers. How dare you imagine your counterfeit marriage grants you superior status?' She jabbed a finger at me, hatred blazing from her. 'I have no doubt that my brother's death is your doing. In this very attic room, you plotted to kill his child, but instead you killed my brother. I do not know how you did it, but I will make you pay for your evil. We will decide how best to deal with you once we have mourned my brother. Father and I will go to church – a place you refuse to set foot – and keep vigil. Together, his real family will pray for the repose of Earnest's soul. But this is not over, Rose Driver. This is far from over.'

❧

Earnest hadn't been dead a week when Minister Leaton arrived at my door, holding up a key. Was he setting me free? He was clad in his church robes so it must be Sunday morning. Did he expect me to attend church? My heart bolted at the thought. Why would they make me go to church now? A memorial service for Earnest, possibly. Whatever the reason, it could work in my favour. Assuming my reaction was the same as on that Easter Sunday all those years ago, a visit to church might rid me of this child. It could be my final chance.

Minister Leaton beckoned me to follow him along the landing. It was so long since I'd walked anywhere other than inside the small confines of my room that my legs were stiff and I struggled to keep up. As we approached the door to the staircase, Minister Leaton took my arm and escorted me down the stairs. Outside, the sky was overcast and the air damp with rain ready to fall, but it was good being in the open air again, even when Patience joined us, holding a cross almost as big as she was.

'Rose,' said Minister Leaton, tightening his grip on my arm, 'you are carrying my late son's child, or that is what I have been led to believe. But lately, I have been made aware of some dubious practices carried out by you. These practices, compounded by the revelation that your grandmother was hanged as a witch by the authorities, and that your mother was accused alongside her, concern me greatly–'

I tried to shake him off to tell him that these were just lies made up by Tilly but he held my arm harder and looked at me closely.

'Regardless of what you choose to believe or have been told by your family, your mother and her mother were both accused of witchcraft. I have questioned Spinster Green under oath. As a result, I must put you to the test and church you. If there is badness in you, we need to drive it out, not just for your sake but for the sake of whatever is in your belly. Patience has given me cause to suspect that the child may not be my son's but a changeling introduced into you by sinister means. If the child is my son's he will survive the ordeal by church and will be all the stronger for it, and if not, my family will be spared from an evil influence on our house. This will go better for you if you do not fight me.'

'I promise not to struggle, Minister Leaton. If you'll permit me, I'll walk into church myself. The child in my belly is your son's. Tilly's lying to you. My grandmother was no witch. My mother was no witch. I am no witch. Please, let me walk into church and prove it to you.'

He looked surprised by this and slowly loosened his grip on my arm.

'Very well, but be warned that if you try to run, I will seize you once again.'

'I won't run. You have my word.'

Even if I'd wanted to, my legs were no longer trustworthy and my belly knocked me off balance, so I wouldn't get too far. Obediently, I turned and started walking towards the church. This wouldn't be too difficult. I'd just put one foot in front of the other and keep going.

Above me the leaden sky pressed down as I progressed towards the church, its door standing open like a mouth ready to swallow me.

The Churching of Widow Leaton

PATIENCE

My father had not been himself since the news of Earnest's death reached us, and I was far from my usual ebullient self. We quarrelled when Father told me of his intent to advise my mother about the loss of her son. As we were ignorant of her whereabouts, he insisted upon writing to my maternal grandmother, certain that Granny Barker would know her daughter's address and contact her on his behalf. For my part, I believed Mother had forfeited the right to know anything concerning either of her children when she absconded, but weakened by sorrow, Father sat at his desk to compose a letter.

In the first bloom of grief, I had lashed out at Rose Driver, blaming her for conjuring to end my brother's life. Whilst I believed her a witch, her powers would not be great enough to reach across the sea and kill so many men. My critical faculties had been blunted by shock. Of course, the blame for Earnest's early demise belonged to our mother, whose actions had abbreviated his life. Were it not for her wanton behaviour, he would be tucked safely into a wealthy parish and married to the second-eldest daughter of his prosperous benefactor. Instead, his comfortable living was withdrawn, and he settled for the naval chaplaincy that had been the death of him. Even after our all-night vigil, Earnest's death did not seem real, and without his body to bury, I doubted it ever would. To me, he was still alive at sea, giving counsel to young men sent to war, their ship sailing forever onwards.

After hearing our tidings, Thomas Verger visited to offer his condolences and asked us to examine some of his handiwork in the churchyard. There stood a cross, cut from yew, planed and polished. Although my brother was not lying there, it would give us somewhere to visit and remember him. The simple cross bore Earnest's name and the dates of his birth and death. There was a sorrowfully brief period between these two dates. Father sank to his knees, heedless of the damp and rotting leaves, running his fingers over the numerals that measured his son's life, praying for the repose of his soul. I would allow him to appreciate this memorial for a time but not for too long.

'This is a touching gesture,' I said, 'if a little rustic, but it is not an original idea, is it?'

'No, Miss Leaton,' said Thomas Verger, 'it's not. Me da built something similar for me when he thought me lost at sea, so I've followed his example.'

My innocent father was so deep in prayer, it seemed a shame to disabuse him, but I could not in all good conscience allow him to wallow in ignorance.

'Of course, there is another instance of this type of proxy grave, is there not? Father, you are perhaps not aware of the marker for Anne Chandler, the maternal grandmother of Earnest's widow.'

At this, my father addressed Verger. 'There is a cross here dedicated to a woman hanged as a witch?'

We waited, silence having considerable utility in prompting confessions from the reluctant. The sexton swallowed and looked at the manse, mindful that any admission would have consequences for his natural daughter.

'Aye, for Annie Chandler, because she's buried in Newcastle...'

He trailed off, unable or unwilling to betray his daughter's corrupted lineage, so I came to his rescue.

'Anne Chandler's remains lie in an unmarked grave in St Andrews of Newcastle because she was executed for consorting with the devil almost quarter of a century ago.'

Prior to her wedding, my sister-in-law had kissed her fingertips and touched them to that cross and those next to it. At the time, it had suggested a sentimental tribute, but this seemingly innocent gesture evidently hid a more diabolical intent. The bride went to her wedding with an invocation to a pair of witches on her fingertips, and one of those fingers next received my grandmother's gold ring.

I saw realisation dawn in Father's eyes. 'So in this plot of land – hallowed land, at that – you erected a monument to a condemned woman? A cross, of all things.'

Father did not give Verger a chance to affirm this state of affairs and stormed across the churchyard to uproot the blasphemous cross from the soil. He lugged it through the lych gate to the outside of the north boundary where he laid it on the ground. Had this marker been fashioned into any other shape, he might have taken an axe to it or burnt it to ashes. The sexton watched my father but did not speak. What was Verger thinking, asking a man in the depths of grief to treat his precious son in the same fashion as an executed witch? The sexton would be fortunate to retain his post, but luckily for him, Father was so distraught that his mind was elsewhere. This frantic removal of the cross reassured me that my father's heart had hardened since his intervention with the housekeeper in Ely. He would not let sympathy get the better of him again. This time, he would not interfere and justice would take its course.

In the ensuing days, my father took to spending more and more time in his writing corner, head bowed, sighing deeply, berating himself for forcing his son to marry. Then he would pore over his Bible and scribble in his breviary, occasionally pausing to contemplate the ceiling. Often, he prayed for Earnest's child – if indeed it was Earnest's child – and beseeched God to save his soul and not allow it to be polluted by his mother's wickedness. He was so exhausted by grief and fear that when I made my suggestion, he acceded without complaint. As with so much in life, timing was all.

❧

My sister-in-law readily agreed to enter the church, which surprised me. Of course, she hoped it would kill the unborn foetus and release the corrupt soul to her dark master, and in return, he would increase her malevolent powers. By entering the church, she hoped to harness the forthcoming terror for her own ends. Courtesy of our loose-lipped servant, I knew the Drivers did not attend church because the cuckoo in their nest could not attend church. Green had reported Rose Driver's visit on the Easter Sunday just over a year after her mother's death. On entering the narthex – or the porch as Green insisted on calling it – *Rosie* became hysterical. It must have been something to witness, because from that day to this, no Driver had set foot inside church again. Curiously, being such blatant sabbath-breakers did not affect their local standing. The Drivers remained prosperous and their neighbours stayed on good terms with them. This would never have happened in Ely where we could rely on parishioners to shun anyone who did not conform.

Assuming Green's intelligence was accurate, Widow Leaton would be so overcome by fear on entering church that she would lose her child. This would benefit my family by ridding us of any future obligation. In the process, it would release a tainted soul, so I stood ready, bearing the processional cross. Although cumbersome, it would provide an element of protection to us and stave off any unholy intervention before we entered the church.

Although the witch had agreed to enter under her own volition and walked through the gabled entrance without so much as a backwards glance, once she set foot in the narthex, she faltered and sat down on the bench, bewildered, panting like a dog, unwilling to move again. Father drew her upright, and wrapped his arm tightly about her, sweeping her towards the church door. Now reluctant to enter, she tried to shrug him off but he continued walking her forwards. As she approached the open door, she dug in her heels, quaking. Undeterred, my father simply lifted her bodily into the air.

'Suppose I carry you, vixen,' he shouted, 'you will be churched. Only inside the house of God can we determine whether you are a hag and what you carry in your belly.'

The witch flailed, bracing her hands and feet against the jambs but these efforts failed to slow my father down and he simply turned to the side and hefted her through the door head-first and into the nave. Upon crossing the threshold, it was as though lightning forked through her and she arced, screeching and twisting her torso, clawing at the pews as she passed, desperately trying to find purchase. All to no avail because Father was filled with righteous fury, so all the endeavours of the witch and her dark master did not impede his progress and he staggered onwards. Fear affected all my sensibilities but I could not let Father down, so I redoubled my grip on the heavy cross and followed him.

Her ungodly cries echoed in the holy space. My breath was shallow and my heart pounded as if Satan's fist squeezed it. Father paused at the altar, the veins in his temple bulging with the strain of raising a pregnant woman onto it, sweat haling from him, but he would not cease in the fight to reveal the truth. As he forced her onto the altar, she clawed at her own face, so her blood mingled with her tears, and the resultant vile fluid dripped onto the altar cloth. Surely this was a summons to her dark master to protect his son, so I applied the cross to her belly. The touch of that most powerful symbol stilled the wretched woman and she fought no more. Father had just begun to say the Lord's Prayer when our holy work was interrupted by a clattering of feet on the flagstones.

'Get your hands off Rose,' shouted Thomas Verger, stampeding down the nave towards the chancel, with no regard for being in the house of God.

When neither of us made a move, the sexton simply prised Father's fingers from his captive, not caring if he fractured a bone, and shoved him so roughly that he fell to the floor and lay there quivering. Although restrained only by the cross, the witch lay quiet, lost in her dark reverie.

Thomas Verger lifted the cross off her and thrust it at me. With no concern for his spiritual safety, he folded his daughter into his arms. Beneath her, the linen was smirched with her bodily wastes. The sullied cloth would have to be burnt and the altar cleansed and re-sanctified.

'You cannot do this to Rose, Minister Leaton,' said Verger. 'It's naught short of cruel and it's a wonder you've not killed her and the bairn.'

Evidently, the ignorant man had no idea of his daughter's ambitions when it came to her child and he strode up the aisle, carrying the pregnant witch as easily as if she were made of air.

'Take your bastard, then,' I shouted. 'But I will see my day with her, Mr Verger, I will see my day.'

All Hallows' Eve

ROSE

Tom Verger carried me away from the church and into his home. He kicked the door shut behind him and placed me on a settle beside the fire. The room was small and dim, apart from the firelight, and the closeness of the walls and roof reassured me because I could see every corner of the room.

'Don't make me go back in there,' I pleaded.

'You won't set foot in another church again, Rose. On my life, I give you my word. You're safe here with me.' He crouched down and looked at me closely. 'You've rived your face to shreds. I'd better clean you up so your granny doesn't get upset when she sees you. But first, have a drink. You must have screamed yourself red raw.'

He dipped a ladle into a pitcher and held it to my lips. I drank the cool water, which soothed my ravaged throat. Next, he removed his kerchief, dipped it into the pitcher and cleaned my stinging wounds.

'Ah, Rose,' he said. 'How badly we've all let you down and me most of all.' He eased himself onto a cracket. 'What have those Leatons done to you?'

I didn't know where to begin. Besides, hundreds of thoughts were overwhelming me now, and I had questions of my own. All my life, a grey mass had sealed off life before my mother died from life now. The grey mass was immovable and I'd come to accept that I was too young to remember those precious early days. I'd been fortunate to be loved by so many people, but growing up surrounded by love didn't stop me from missing all that I'd lost. Since childhood, I'd yearned for my mother, trying to glean memories from those who'd known her and whose minds weren't shut off like mine.

Before today, my earliest memory had been Easter Sunday when I was three or four. It was warm and sunny and I rode up the hill on Da's shoulders. When we reached the lych gate, I slid to the ground. Da and Granny each took a hand and walked me to church, but as soon as we set foot inside the porch, I couldn't take another step and screamed the place down.

Da carried me straight home. From that day forwards, we never went to church again and nobody talked about it. Yet, I could enter the manse to visit Reverend Foster and the graveyard to visit the Vergers' hut. I stayed outside for services, and even the Leatons had accommodated me for Da's burial and the wedding. All my life, people had helped me so I didn't have to go into church, and no one had questioned this till today, when – for reasons unknown to me – the Leatons decided to take me into the church.

At first, I'd wanted to go in and walked willingly into the porch. But then I remembered that place and not from the sunny Easter Sunday of my childhood. A wave of panic engulfed me and I'd sat down heavily on the wooden bench, my breath coming in quick gasps as memory after memory surfaced. I'd slept on this bench once. That was before. Then I recalled huddling underneath it. That was after. But before what and after what were not yet clear to me. When I was still grappling with these piecemeal memories, Minister Leaton picked me up and dragged me into the belly of the church, and I'd fought him with every ounce of strength I possessed to stop him taking me deeper. I kicked and screeched, grabbing whatever was at hand but naught slowed him and he threw me down on the altar and his daughter pinned me there with a large cross. There I lay, frozen, immersed in the depths of the shadows that had haunted my childhood dreams. I was wide awake but the shadows surrounded me, closing in, and I clawed at them, trying to escape, sobbing and losing control of myself.

In the safety of Tom Verger's shack, I lay wrapped in a thick rug and gazed into the flames, piecing together what had come back to me from that distant Candlemas night of my early childhood. First, I remembered being woken by a mouse scrabbling in my hair. Something heavy covered me, which smelt of my mother. Her cloak. I'd kicked it off me, afraid it was filled with mice. Even though I was wearing my clothes and boots, it was freezing. Then I realised this wasn't my basket at home. Waking alone in the dark in a strange place disturbed me and set me whingeing, too afraid to move or call out. My fingers were wrapped around a wooden toy. Gyb. Just like our real cat. Stroking the toy comforted me and as my eyes adjusted in the darkness, the porch revealed itself to me.

More often than not, my mother had fetched me out of church mid-service when I wouldn't settle, when even playing with Granny's fancy thimble didn't distract me. That Candlemas night all those years ago, the air held a trace of ice and snow. Now, despite the warmth from Tom Verger's fire, I shivered at the recollection.

When the screams reached me in the church porch, it had taken me a while to realise it was my mother screaming. She'd often wept, but she'd never screamed. I sat up and lowered myself, unsure of the drop, and as soon as my feet reached the ground, I crept towards the terrible noise. A long strip of light flickered from the floor to the ceiling and drew me towards it. A door. Slightly ajar. Not strong enough to push it open, I'd peered through the narrow opening and into the church.

The flame of a solitary candle bowed in the slight breeze. Its flickering made huge dancing shadows that washed the walls. The screams echoed. A giant loomed over my mother. He raised his dagger. He lowered his dagger. She lay still. The giant dragged a bundle from her. Laid it on the altar. A thin wail. A baby! My mother had told me a baby lived inside her belly, and I'd worried, imagining she'd swallowed it. But the baby wasn't inside her any more and it was wailing. My poor brother didn't manage to draw breath for another wail. The knife flashed and he fell silent.

Now, I remembered it all. The warmth running down my cold legs as I lost control of myself. An invisible hand squeezing my throat, stopping me from crying out. My leaden feet as I walked the few steps backwards and scuttled beneath the bench. Not understanding what I'd seen but afraid of it anyway. Trembling and silent. Cold, wet and afraid. Running footsteps came from outside and I shrank back but someone found me anyway and hauled me out. It was Bill Verger, the kind man who'd given me the wooden cat. He wrapped me in my mother's cloak and carried me down the hill to Granny Driver, singing in my ear all the way, patting me and holding me close to him.

These memories had lain fallow. They'd always been there, but only as black shapes that woke me screaming in the night. Somewhere inside me, I knew what had happened, but my mind had hidden it from me. Thanks to the Leatons churching me earlier today, the grey mass was no more and my past forced itself into my present. How could God allow such an atrocity to pass in a church? Of course, no god could permit that to happen. So there was no God and no heaven. My mother and brother weren't there waiting for me. Instead, they were just bones in the earth.

Finally, I found my voice. 'They died so cruelly, my mother and brother, and I didn't raise so much as a finger to save them.'

Tom slowly shook his head. 'You were only a bit bairn and he was a madman, Rose. You mustn't blame yourself.'

But I did blame myself. I could have cried out or run for help, but instead I'd stood by and watched the slaughter. A great cramp doubled me up, making me afraid that what I'd longed for all these months was coming to pass. Too late, I realised that I didn't want to be rid of my child, just my dread. For so long, I'd believed my mother died in childbirth and fear of dying the same way had dogged me all my life. Finally, I knew different.

'You should have told me the truth, Tom. Someone should have told me.'

'Aye, you're right, Rose, but not when you were a bairn. We were all agreed on that. The Vergers, the Drivers and Reverend Foster. But the years got away from us. It never seemed the right time. I hope you can forgive us. Forgive me.'

It wasn't fair of him to ask forgiveness for such a lie. Because of that lie, I'd almost killed my child to save myself. How would I ever face him? Clutching my middle, I fell back onto the settle and darkness washed over me.

I awoke to find Tom Verger watching over me. Never had a man looked more sorrowful. He encouraged me to drink a bowl of milk and honey.

'In return, will you tell me everything? Please.'

'Aye, Rose. I will.'

When my bowl was empty, he covered my hands with his, and he did tell me everything. From start to finish.

The Accusation

PATIENCE

After the disastrous churching of my sister-in-law, I recommended a hallowing to remove any trace of her unclean presence. Father agreed and we prayed throughout the night, but still the church felt befouled, as well it might after its recent infestation.

Thomas Verger moved his natural daughter to the farmstead, despite my father's fervent wish to keep her at the manse under constant watch. But Elizabeth Driver, dissatisfied with our accommodation of her granddaughter, would not allow us near her.

Father was perturbed by the fact that the pregnancy remained intact. Originally, he had believed that after the churching, a true child of Earnest would prevail, whereas a false child would not. But having seen the desperate state of his daughter-in-law on All Hallows' Eve, he no longer clung to the belief that she carried Earnest's child since the foetus could not be shifted from its mother's womb by any earthly power. Having consulted both his conscience and the Bible, he was now satisfied that the charge of witchcraft was just.

Nowadays, all hope destroyed, he hunched over his desk, gazing at the hills. It was most unlike him, a man who lived for his work. So soon after his bereavement, the prospect of a joyous birth had been stolen from him. Instead of a child named for Earnest to soothe his broken heart, a changeling grew inside his daughter-in-law.

Even Green's culinary skills could not rouse Father these days, and he picked at his food. Never a glutton, he scarcely ate enough to sustain his body and risked following my brother to an early grave. Seeing this hollow man made me ache. Each passing day that accursed woman drew breath insulted him. So it became more urgent than ever to encourage a higher authority to undertake further investigations.

It was a simple task to persuade Father of the need to report matters to his new archdeacon. That venerable man would listen to us and determine a corrective course of action. In his melancholy state, my father was easy to lead – a blessing as time was against us. For every minute he grieved in the manse, the witch lay in the valley, feeding on the fat of the land, the false child drawing strength from her.

With the benefit of hindsight, it was obvious why the Drivers refused to observe the sabbath. Unwittingly, they had invited a viper to nest in the bosom of their family and they had enabled her truancy from church, aided and abetted by the delinquent priest. Whilst my father had returned the parish to some form of rigour, the Drivers continued to flout the law. Needless to say, the winsome Goodwife Driver had played her part, offering my father gifts, thereby making it harder for him to punish his disobedient parishioners.

That we had failed in our original mission would stand us in poor stead with the Church, which meant we might never regain our former living in Ely. Consequently, we would be stuck in this awful dale until we were buried in the churchyard at Mutton Clog. If we were to be allowed home, we must somehow prove ourselves here. So the only way out was to reveal the truth to the authorities, beginning with

Rose Driver's conjury with the dead lamb and culminating in her inability to attend church and her astonishing reaction when forced to do so.

After being reminded once again of all that had transpired, Father needed only a modicum of encouragement from me to write to the archdeacon. All this time, he had believed his daughter-in-law innocent, if a little wayward. But after witnessing the spectacle in the church and learning of her ancestry, he could be in no doubt that she was a consort of the devil. That being the case, he had finally accepted that his daughter-in-law carried in her belly not his grandson but some unholy foetus sired by a servant of hell.

I fastened the letter with Father's clerical seal and summoned Green. I gave her a coin and sent her to find a messenger, with orders not to come back until either she or the missive had reached the cathedral in Durham.

At last, it was beginning.

WINTER

North Gate Gaol

ROSE

The wagon taking me to Durham gave no protection from the elements and winter cut through my clothes. To either side of the road, the wind howled through the bare trees, and I crouched in a corner to protect myself from the lashing sleet as best I could. The journey could kill me and the bairn, if the cold didn't finish us first.

Now that I knew the truth about my mother's death, the terror of dying in childbed had lessened. And since the little stranger in my womb had quickened, he'd felt real to me, always stretching his arms and legs on waking, drumming his hands and feet joyfully whenever I ate something that pleased him. I'd come to know him, and to know someone was halfway to loving them.

But just when I'd begun to love my child, I feared he wouldn't see the light of day because I might not live long enough to reach term. When the sergeants appeared on the brow of the hill at Mutton Clog, I knew they were there for me, on account of my churching. They'd wasted not a minute riding down the hill. On seeing them, my grandmother had reached the same conclusion and begged me to plead my belly.

'What would be the point, when they'll simply bide their

time, take my infant from me and hang me anyway? Besides, pleading indicates guilt, doesn't it?'

She patted my hand. 'Aye, but you'd not be in prison, which would spare the bairn and give you a few more months. A lot could change. The Leatons could move on, the Church could forget...'

She'd meant it as a kindness but she was misguided if she thought a plea would save me. The Church had the longest of memories, with the Leatons a close second.

'Patience Leaton is determined, Granny, and she'll not rest till she's brought me low. So I have no choice but to go to trial and tell the truth.'

❧

When we arrived in Durham, the horses trotted over a stone bridge and turned sharply up a steep cobbled street, almost jouncing me free. The cart was hemmed in on both sides by tall buildings with pointed gables. Dusk was falling but I managed to make out the vast wall of stone looming in front of me. The wall fronted a castle and behind it towered the cathedral. I'd never seen anything grander than the church and the manse but they'd be lost against these buildings with all their towers and turrets. Set into the wall was a wide gateway and when the cart drew to a halt under its arch, I was grateful for the shelter from the sleet.

A hulking fellow with coarse features came out to meet us, his jaw hanging slackly in an attempt at a smile. He nodded to the sergeants, who unloaded me, waiting them to hand me into his custody till he addressed me.

'Welcome to North Gate Gaol,' said the man. 'I'm the turnkey here, and will pay no heed to your magical dealings. I make no exceptions for women, so expect no gentle treatment on account of your sex.'

Hunched inside my wet clothes, I hoped there'd be a fire

inside the prison to get myself dry, but this man enjoyed keeping me outside in the cold.

'Make no mistake,' said the turnkey, 'gaol has been my occupation, man and boy, and I've seen every form of mischief going. Presently, I'll admit you, and if you keep your nose clean, I may one day release you. Shadow me closely and watch your step. You wouldn't be the first to fall in here, though it looks to me as if you've fallen already.'

He winked at this crude remark and led me through a side door into the gaol, holding the lantern to light his own path. Inside was darker than the street and I hurried to stay close behind him in the dim glow. Underfoot the stones were slippery and to my sides the walls were damp and slimy.

As we journeyed deeper, a stench arose that was worse than any byre at the end of winter – the result of many people held in close captivity. Shouts and screams and bangs and thumps echoed around me. I dreaded to think what caused them and yearned to be back at the farmstead. Even the Leatons' attic would be preferable to this dingy midden.

'You'll dwell all alone, Leaton,' said the turnkey. 'You cannot stop with the other women for fear you turn them to the dark side.' He paused, held up the lantern and examined me. 'Just be glad it's my quiet time and I've a separate cell for you. Otherwise, you'd be down in the great hole, and there's not a damper or darker place in the whole gaol. Because you have to be kept apart from the other women, you'll not be able to sing for your supper, but a few days on water soup should do no harm till your people fetch you some provisions and raise the money for your keep. Be grateful the assizes aren't too far off. Plenty of lasses in your boat have perished awaiting their date.'

I shied away from him, wondering what lay ahead of me in this place, and whether I would see Granny or May again.

'Please, sir, when is my hearing?'

He blew out his cheeks. 'Couple of months, give or take.

Six weeks. Closer to seven, by my reckoning. Your days are numbered, Leaton, and you'll not celebrate Christmas in North Gate. One way or another.'

I quailed at the thought of being dead so soon and my child with me. No more than fifty dawns left on this earth if the trial found against me.

'Give over dawdling, lass.' With that, the man dragged me by the arm down a murky passage, stopping short to unlock a door. He shoved me through it. When my eyes adjusted to the murk, I found myself in a low room no bigger than our old sty. Behind me, the door slammed shut and the key turned. So he'd gone and left me. What had I ever done to my cruel sister-in-law to deserve this? Hopefully, the justice would see sense and realise that my accuser was just an unhappy young woman, raving at the untimely passing of her brother.

In truth, I set little store on my innocence saving me. Grandmother Chandler was innocent, yet the Newcastle justice had failed to see sense and he'd condemned her to hang, and almost my mother with her. It was a dark notion, but now I knew my mother's true fate, hanging might have been a kinder end and would have spared her from witnessing her son's slaughter.

As for my own fate, I hardly knew which was worse. A swift death by hanging. Or a drawn-out death caused by disease and deprivation. For now, it was best not to think about it so I'd try to sleep and reserve my strength. Nearby, there were scratchings and I folded myself into my cloak. It was still sodden, but it was the only protection left to me. All my life, I'd been sturdy, sensible, hard-working and honest. If naught else, those qualities would stand me in good stead. There were two things I mustn't do at any cost. Plead my belly and as good as admit guilt. Or lose hope. I removed the little wooden cat from my bodice and ran my thumb over him. Gyb had comforted me as a child and perhaps he would do so now.

ॐ

Never a good sleeper, I was awake more and more, my senses no longer my own till I wondered if I *was* guilty of whatever they were accusing me of. Waking so frequently and it being so dark made it impossible to work out how long had passed. There was a window a little bigger than that in the Leatons' attic, but it was so smeared with grime that no light came in. The darkness here was different to that of the attic. Up there, I could look at the stars or the moon. Here, I could look only at darkness as morning was barely lighter than night. I relied on my bodily movements to measure the passage of time, but without food and water, they were changing. Already, my child moved within me less and less.

Despite my best intentions, hope leached from me. I was very much aware that each passing minute was one nearer to freedom, but it could also be one nearer to death. And if no one gave me any water soon, I wouldn't last the week, never mind till Yuletide. During my captivity at the manse, Tilly kept me fed and watered, though not like she had at home, and I'd gone hungry more than once. But now I knew real thirst and hunger, and feared what it would do to my child, let alone me. I tried to separate my mess from my sleeping corner, but in such a small space it was difficult. Although muffled, the screams were horrible and ripped through the prison at all hours. When the men screamed, their deep voices broke. I'd not been harmed yet, but that could change.

ॐ

It could have been the next day, or the one after, but a shaft of light shone on me and I shut my eyes against it. This wasn't sunshine though, because it brought with it the loud roar from the main body of the gaol. Someone had opened the door, and I prayed they were bringing me water and food. I squinted at the doorway, unaccustomed to the light and there stood an elderly woman, warmly wrapped in a grey worsted frock and shawl, holding a large covered basket. She was saying something. At first, I couldn't hear her over the gaol racket, but after a while her words resolved into a list of wares: bread, milk, ale and cheese. I had no coin to pay her but perhaps she held some sympathy for my rumbling stomach because she began to question me.

'What parish are your people from? Will they be in to visit you?'

I had no idea when Granny and May would come, or even if they knew where I'd been taken.

'Cat got your tongue, lass?'

'Sorry, madam. My people are from Mutton Clog.'

She cackled. 'Never heard of it. Where does it lie?'

'It lies in Derwentdale.'

'Ah well, if your people do pay a visit, pray they leave you some coin. I'll be seeing you. Mind yourself, lass.'

'Wait! Please don't leave me. I need some water...'

But she took herself away and closed the door, leaving me in the dark with only the distant screams and shouts for company. If the turnkey came back, I'd beg him to move me in with some other prisoners because being here by myself would soon send me mad if I didn't die of thirst or hunger before then.

My limbs were heavy and my neck hardly strong enough to hold up my head. I kept nodding off, only to be woken by a cramping in my middle. Cold to the bone, I'd have willingly exchanged my soul for a quart of water, a bite to eat and an unbroken sleep. My body was so heavy and the damp stone so hard that I felt every bone and my throat ached from thirst.

Again and again, my thoughts turned to my own bed, with its feather tick, warmed each night with a hot stone wrapped in rabbit skin. So much love and care from Granny and May. How welcome it was after a hard day on the hills to sink into such softness, to rest my face against the smooth linen of my bolster, to draw the heavy quilt over me and melt away into sleep. Never had I truly appreciated these women's kindness till today.

When sleep finally took me, I dreamt of being curled up in a small basket at the foot of my parents' bed, but instead of snuggling, I was sulking and demanding to play with my poppet. But my mother wouldn't allow me to get up. Instead, she wept and begged me to sleep. Now, I would do as she asked and sleep. Sleep forever if I could. Find my mother and dry her tears.

The Mourners

PATIENCE

My letter to the archdeacon had achieved the desired effect. Sergeants were despatched immediately from Durham. They arrived on the brow of the hill in a horse-drawn wagon, signalling their intention to take a prisoner with them. Despite the freezing sleet, Green ran outside and I followed at a more sedate pace, keen to observe. The two sergeants paused and pointed down to the valley.

Green turned to me, aghast. 'Have they come for Rosie?'

'I sincerely hope they have so justice might be done and peace can prevail in the parish.'

My father came out to join us just as Thomas Verger left his shack. The sexton's face was ashen when he addressed us.

'What have you done to my lass? What have you done?'

I merely shrugged, unwilling to waste words on him.

The sexton looked sick to the soul, which was to be expected from a man related by blood to the witch, but my father wore a similarly stricken look. Verger said no more and ran off to the valley. What he hoped to achieve, I could not begin to guess.

With the rest of my household, I stood and gazed at the scene unfolding below. The Drivers' door opened and the elder widow stood, arms folded, while the sergeants addressed her. But their clubs proved unnecessary as their prisoner soon presented herself.

Verger ran swiftly, considering his advanced years, but not swiftly enough. His daughter pushed past her womenfolk and climbed unaided into the wagon. The sergeant flicked the reins and the horses started up the hill. Verger ran alongside, arguing with the sergeants until one flicked him with his horsewhip and he fell back. Undeterred, he got straight back on his feet and gave chase again, but once the horses reached the flat, they gathered speed. Verger's efforts were hopeless and he stopped and stared after his departing daughter, hands on knees, panting, impotent in the wake of the law.

'Patience,' said my father, 'it might be wise for you to retire indoors.'

'I have nothing to fear when I am doing the Lord's work.'

'It was not a request. Go indoors when you are told.'

Unaccustomed to being spoken to in this way, I obeyed, but Father's order was quite unnecessary because Verger was not coming back to berate me. Instead, he returned to the valley, no doubt to visit Widow Driver to collude and conspire.

There was no more to do, so I allowed Green to shepherd me to the manse. Later, I would slip across to the church to give thanks to God for listening to my prayers and sending his messengers to arrest the witch. All that remained for me to do now was to wait.

❦

Father had fallen silent since the sergeants removed the witch from our midst. His reticence on the matter cast a shadow on my jubilance and even Green went about veiled in sorrow. They must not feel pity in their hearts because my sister-in-law was merely a hollow vessel, inhabited by an unclean spirit.

Our parishioners also failed to share my joy, and regardless of the weather, many of them were to be seen coming and going from the Drivers' farmstead. Without asking leave, our sexton set off in a wagon driven by Farmer Johnson and accompanied by Blenkinsop and the two Widows Driver. With them, they carried bundles and baskets. Provisions and goods no doubt intended to prolong the life of the witch.

We must investigate anyone associating with a suspected witch. It might behove me to look more deeply into their behaviour for there may be other witches in our midst.

'Perhaps it would be worth—'

Father put up a hand to silence me. 'No, Patience. You have done quite enough. More than enough. Earnest's widow has been taken away from us...'

How quickly moved to compassion was my frail parent.

'Please do not think of that woman as Earnest's widow. Remember that she carries within her an infant sired by the dark saint. Yes, she looked pathetic. And yes, the journey to Durham would not have been easy for her in an open wagon in all that weather. But do not lose faith. Remember all that she has done.'

I took my journal from my apron pocket and flicked back to my jottings from the early days of my suspicions. The skinned lamb. The cut hand. The blood pact. The storm raising. My injury. The seduction of my brother. The attempt at killing an unborn child. And chief amongst them all, the inability to enter church. I tapped a finger down the list of evidence to remind my father but he showed no interest.

'Put down your book, Patience, and write no more. I worry that committing your thoughts to paper makes them more tangible than they might otherwise appear. Your accusations seem to take on a life of their own. It may be too late for that poor girl. Perhaps there is time to retract…'

My father was no longer in possession of his wits. He had witnessed the churching of my sister-in-law, which confirmed absolutely her involvement with the profane. Fortunately, my father was little-known in Durham, so he would hold no sway. That woman was now beyond his influence and her fate rested entirely in the hands of the authorities.

Word arrived from Durham that the next assizes were due to occur in the third week of December, which was unusually late in the year and during Advent to boot. So long to wait for my sister-in-law to get her comeuppance. There would be little to do on these dark afternoons so I planned to revise and rehearse my deposition. In Ely, I had charged into the situation like a dog at broth. Older and wiser now, I knew the importance of preparation. I was in my chamber, declaiming from my journal when there was a knock at my door.

'Green, are you unable to discern that I am busy, or unwilling?'

'Sorry, madam. Begging your pardon. But I thought you might like to know that there are two strange women at Earnest's grave, and Tom Verger is talking to them. Two women, not of this parish, one elderly and one less so. Well-built and well-dressed, both.'

O, it could not be! I went to the window and peered down. There, kneeling in the snow at my brother's marker, muffled and swathed within an inch of their lives, were Mother and Granny. The shock of seeing them left me quite faint. How dare my mother pollute our new parish? Even my love for Granny Barker would not soften my heart towards her promiscuous daughter.

Father was praying, so with luck, they would be gone before he came out and saw them. And I must get them away from our sexton, who laboured under the impression that my mother had expired during childbirth.

'Green, go to the church and distract Minister Leaton. Do not announce these visitors to him. I shall deal with them. Go through the scullery door so they do not notice you. Be quick.'

We trotted down the stairs at double-time, and as I unlatched the front door, Green slipped away on her errand through the back. I raced to my brother's proxy grave, where Thomas Verger regarded me. He said nothing, but his contempt was apparent. I would speak to Father and insist that he release the man from his post. In the meantime, there was a more pressing matter to address. Kneeling in front of me, soberly dressed in black, was the woman who gave birth to Earnest and me. A stranger for the best part of a year but the only change in her was the grey smudge beneath each eye.

'Patience.' A sob broke in her throat as she opened her arms to me.

I spared her a curt nod. 'You and your curate are fortunate that my father gave up his rights as cuckold. No one would have blamed him for seeking retribution, given the adverse effects your behaviour had on his reputation and his living. Not to mention what you did to my brother.'

Now she did sob. 'Have mercy, Patience. Your brother has died and I am in despair.'

So, some misplaced maternal grief for her favourite child – her only child, as far as she was concerned – had fetched her.

Granny Barker fixed me with her most fierce look.

'Patience Leaton, you'll not speak to your mother in such tones. She can't be blamed for leaving a cold marriage in search of warmth. Keep a decent tongue in your head, if not for the love of your mother then for the love of God. Remember the fifth commandment, girl.'

Quite why anyone should honour a wanton confounded me. God would certainly not expect unfaithful absentees to be included in the command to honour one's parents.

Before I could argue my point, I saw Father hurrying over, followed by a breathless Green, still urging him to remain in the church. She had failed miserably in her mission, but she had done her best.

'Agnes?' said Father in a tremulous voice as he picked up the hem of his cassock and rushed towards her in a most unseemly manner, our servant bringing up the rear.

'Hector,' said Mother, 'I came north as soon as I received your letter. Oh, it's too much to bear. Our poor boy.'

Granny put her arm around her daughter's shoulders to brace her.

'Patience, stop standing there,' said Father, 'and take Agnes and Granny inside. You can't keep them outside in this weather.'

Typically, he failed to notice that his sole remaining child was outside in her indoor garments. I walked to the manse, holding the door open until everyone entered and Green shut it behind her.

Mother made her appeal. 'Dearest Hector I need to visit our son's chamber. To rest my hand where he last rested his head....'

Her knees buckled and Father caught her and steered her into the parlour where he settled her into his chair. He looked at her for a long whilst until she recovered herself and I did not like what I saw in his eyes.

'Agnes, our daughter will take you upstairs to Earnest's chamber while Green makes a meal.' I made no move, so he raised his voice. 'Go when you are told, Patience. Do not disobey me.'

Agnes had not been here two minutes and already I was

demoted to being some kind of lackey. It would not do to argue though, because Granny was a termagant and not above giving me a thrashing, even at my age.

'Come with me,' I said. Father caught my eye, so I began again. 'Come with me, *Mother*, and I will show you Earnest's chamber.'

I climbed the stairs and she followed me, sniffling with every step. Someone who loved her son enough to visit his grave should not have deserted him. When we arrived outside his chamber, I paused. No Leaton had entered this room since the news of Earnest's death. Green had gone in after his departure to make the bed, and I suspected her of sneaking in there to weep on more than one occasion.

Now it was my mother's turn. Her heels skittered over the dark wood floor. Upon reaching the bed, she removed her left glove, pulled back the mustard brocade eiderdown and smoothed her hand across the bolster.

'I dreamt of him. Earnest. He came to me. Your brother emerged in the distance, walking slowly towards me. Although I held out my arms, he didn't move or smile or make any sound. I ran to him, but no matter how fast, I couldn't reach him because he moved further and further away, even though his feet were still.'

She drew a juddering breath. Why tell me this? Was it some sort of prophetic dream? Maybe she was half-witch herself. It would explain a good deal. I made to leave the chamber, but she kept on.

'Earnest held his hand to his temple and showed me his injury. Though very far away, I saw blood seeping from him, his shattered bones. I hurried to him again, but grey mist shrouded him until he vanished, all sight of him lost. Although I could see for miles in all directions, there was no sign of him.'

A look of pure agony suffused her and without asking my permission, she slid into the bed and lay in the very place my brother would have lain. She cried so much she almost choked on her tears. The bolster would be sopping. Did she not comprehend that her loose ways had cost my brother his life? For a time, I had blamed his widow, but really, the blame rested squarely on my mother's shoulders.

I could not stand to witness this performance – and performance it certainly was – for another second, so I retreated downstairs.

Granny was out of her travelling clothes and sat at the table with Father, the pair of them dining on pea soup, whilst Green hovered anxiously in the background. Little wonder after the naive girl sold me information about her former bedmate in exchange for the possibility of becoming the future Goodwife Leaton. In the meanwhile, upstairs was the original, far from dead. Instead, very much alive, all plump and contrite, demure in her mourning weeds. After her desertion, Father had stiffened his resolve against her, but in their joint sorrow at the loss of Earnest, a reconciliation looked increasingly possible.

When my mother came downstairs, her eyes were reddened and puffed, her hair in disarray, and I noticed a worrying softening in my father.

'Sit down, Agnes, please. Spinster Green will fetch you some nourishing soup.'

Green quickly obliged and after spending some time arranging the dish on the table, she curtsied prettily. Granny eyed her.

'Is there no scullery work to be getting on with, girl?'

Our servant flushed and scurried away, and Granny returned her attention to the table, appearing an inch or two taller than earlier. She was in fighting spirit and I dreaded to think what this might mean for my parents' marriage.

'Patience,' asked my grandmother in a voice nothing short of imperious, 'have you no errands to run?'

'No, Granny, I always complete my errands immediately upon waking.'

At this, she humphed and filled her mouth with bread. She wanted rid of me so she could interfere – her favourite pastime.

Mother held a spoonful of soup to her lips with an unsteady hand.

'In his letter, your father mentioned Earnest's widow and child.' Tears threatened again and she blinked them away. 'Might it be possible to meet her while I'm here? I should so love to be a grandmother. Nothing can bring Earnest back, but perhaps his child...'

Father looked at me, almost pleading, but I would not spare her feelings. Better by far to be honest.

'There have been several developments since that letter.'

'Developments?' She placed her spoon in her dish with a clank and Father winced.

I took a deep breath. It would be kinder to inform her quickly rather than prolong the agony. 'Earnest's widow is indeed carrying a child, but we have reason to believe that it is not his.'

Mother pushed away her plate, hardly daring to ask the question on her lips. Of course, she assumed I referred to adultery, given her own guilty conscience in that regard.

'The woman is a witch, and what she carries in her belly is an infant with an unholy provenance. You are not destined to be a grandmother, I am afraid to inform you.'

Her soft white hand fluttered at her throat as she fought for breath. 'A witch? Hector, is this true? Did you permit our son to marry a witch?'

Father did not get the chance to reply, because Granny thumped the table, causing the pea soup to shiver in the porcelain bowls.

'Witches be damned!'

I gaped at her profanity. No wonder my mother had such slack morals when her own mother was not afraid to blaspheme in the presence of a man of God. Rather than castigate her, Father merely lowered his head and prayed.

'Patience Leaton,' bellowed Granny. 'What have you been up to? Don't you think your parents have enough on their plates without you imagining witchcraft at every turn?' She paused to mop her mouth. 'When I think of what you did to that poor housekeeper of yours and her unborn child. Hector, what were you thinking of, letting the girl get up to her old tricks again? You should have put a stop to this nonsense the second it started.'

It was just as well my grandmother did not know the paternity of the Ely infant because if she learnt I was responsible for finishing off the son of her favourite grandchild, she would string me up herself.

Despite being of one accord with his mother-in-law on the matter of the dead housekeeper, Father disliked being berated, especially by Granny Barker, and his lips were compressed into a straight line. Good. Now that he was cross, he would not be so easily gulled by her into forgiving my adulterous mother.

Visitations

ROSE

A shaft of dim light disturbed me and I tried to raise my head.

'Afternoon, Mutton Clog. Still in the land of the living?'

My mouth tasted acrid and my head swam, leaving me nauseous, so even the faint light through the door hurt my eyes. It took a while to work out that the voice was real and not talking to me from my dreams. The wares woman again.

'Not speaking, eh? If that's how it is, I'll be off. Got better ways to waste my hours than trudging through the snow to wait on you.'

'No,' I said. 'Please wait. Don't go.'

'Ah, it lives. Your folks been in yet?'

Had they? I'd seen them in my broken dreams so often, I couldn't be sure.

'It's hard to tell.'

'Best way to tell is if they've left you some coin. Pat your pinny pocket. Have they?'

My pocket was as empty as my stomach. 'No, not yet.'

'Often the way with a lass in your condition. Some families are glad to see the back of an expectant widow. Another two mouths to feed, and no one wants that. In normal circumstances, you could work for your bait, but the turnkey's afraid to put you near the other women in case you cause a contagion.'

I shuffled closer to her in the vain hope that she might take pity and give me some of her wares.

'If they've not been in yet, it's doubtful they ever will. But unlike many around these parts, I'm a decent person and wouldn't want to see you fade away, so you can have some bread and milk. What have you got to barter?'

All I had was what I stood up in. What could I manage without?

'My pinny,' I said. 'You can have my apron.'

'Oh, lass,' she clucked. 'There's no call for pinnies, especially mucky white linen ones. I'll save us both some time. What's needed in this place is warmth and protection. Have you anything of that order?'

What could be sacrificed that wouldn't hurt me too much? My stockings. I could do without them. It wasn't as if I needed to walk anywhere so my feet wouldn't get too sore when my boots were made of sheepskin.

'You can take my stockings. My people are farmers, so it's our own wool. My grandmother knitted them and she's famed throughout the bishopric for her skill with the stocking needles.'

'Oh, is she? Warms my cockles to hear it. I'll wager this famous granny of yours has outfitted you in the finest wool cloak and good leather boots and all.'

I was about to correct her about my boots but realised what her game was. With the damp and the cold, I couldn't part with my cloak and boots so soon.

'Oh, my cloak is an old hand-me-down, held together with patches. The same goes for my boots – they let in more than they keep out.'

'Ah, a pity, that. For now, I'll settle on your stockings and your pinny. In return, you can have a flask of milk. If you're wanting bread and all, it'll cost you your cloak and boots.'

I had to stand my ground to get the best bargain

possible. 'That doesn't seem fair. Wool stockings and a linen pinny for a quart of milk.'

'Even less fair for the pint of milk you'll be getting, lass, but milk is far from cheap even in the summer months, and it's a rarer commodity at this time of year since I cannot draw it from the well as if it were water. Listen, hinny, you're not haggling down the market, so decide what's more important to you – the clothes on your back, or your body and soul. Pinny and stockings for a pint of milk. Not another word on the matter.'

She watched me take off my stockings and pinny, then passed me a stoppered flask. Barely half-full and nowhere near a pint. Without pausing to consider whose lips might have touched the flask before mine, I took a sip. Years of feeding cade lambs told me not to be greedy. My stomach contained nothing but air and supping too fast would fetch the milk straight up so I took it slowly. Far from fresh, and thinned with water, it was the sweetest drink of my life. My stockings alone were worth a lot more than a measly few mouthfuls of milk, but however hungry and thirsty, I mustn't show my desperation. The wares woman stood to gain plenty from selling my belongings and when she saw what the stockings fetched, she'd be back. It would be worth holding out for another day to buy twice the amount of bread, and maybe some more milk.

'The pinny's not up to much, lass, but these stockings are canny. Now, I have some day-old bread going begging, if you want to reconsider selling your cloak...'

I kept quiet, though it nearly broke me to deny myself food.

'Suit yourself, Mutton Clog,' she said, and swept out of the door. 'Till the morrow, when you'll be that bit more hungry and a lot more desperate.'

By the time my cell door opened, I was faint with hunger but would not give in straight away and would use what I'd gleaned from watching Granny at the mart.

'Morning, lass,' said the wares woman. 'Ready to sell your cloak? Let's say, half a loaf.'

'A whole one,' I countered, 'and another flask of milk.'

'Drive a hard bargain for a starving prisoner, don't you? I'll have to feel the quality of the cloth first. No arguments.'

I had no choice but to trust her, so I unfastened my cloak and handed it to her. She took her time fingering the rich wool and hefting the weight of it. Already, the cold bit into me, but my need for nourishment outdid my need for warmth.

'Mind,' she said, 'it's a lot dirtier than it was yesterday. Always a problem with undyed wool. Now it's so hacky, it's worth less to me. If you want milk on top of bread, you'll have to make do with half a loaf.'

My heart thumped. Granny would throw a fit at hearing her woollen goods slandered in this way. The wares woman could just walk off with my cloak and there was no way of stopping her. But she'd return for my boots and if she wanted them, she must give keep her side of the bargain.

'A full loaf,' I insisted. 'And a flask of milk. I'm with child and haven't eaten since I got here.'

'You're a wicked lass pulling at my heartstrings with your tales of woe. A loaf it is. A small one, mind. And you'll get your milk since I'm soft-hearted when it comes to bairns.'

I drained the milk from the flask and could have wept when I saw the bread. Barely bigger than my fist and almost as hard as my knuckles. I gnawed on it and chewed as fast as I could. Never in my life had I known hunger like this and it was best to eat it all and not save any for later or the rats would have it. Once she'd gone, I stayed awake as long as possible so sheer exhaustion would help me to sleep later without the benefit of my cloak. When tiredness threatened to overtake me, I curled up, clutching Gyb, my skin shrunken on my limbs and scalp, and all the small hairs on my body standing up.

Someone must come soon. Granny and May wouldn't leave me here to rot. I depended on it because my belly would get the better of me, and the wares woman would take my boots and then my frock, and when that was gone, I dreaded to think what would be next.

⁊

A couple more visits from the wares woman left me shivering in my shift. The little shreds of clothing left to me were no protection and the damp and the bitterness would soon be the death of me. I gazed blankly into the darkness as I circled the cell.

No need to worry any more about keeping my feet clean and dry as they were no longer touching the floor and I was floating. Round and round. Flying even. It was good to fly. Soon I would fly away up and out of here. I laughed and the sound echoed as though many prisoners were in here with me. I cowered away from them, flying no more.

My eyes were closed, but there was light on the other side. It would be lovely to go into the light and not feel afraid or cold or hungry or thirsty ever again. From a distance, a voice called out my name. Was it my mother? No, it sounded like a man's voice. Perhaps it was Da.

'Rose,' said the voice. 'Rose, can you hear me? It's Tom. Tom Verger.'

I struggled to speak and shrank further into myself.

'Rose, it's me, Tom Verger.'

Was Tom Verger dead? Why would he be calling me? With a jolt, I remembered he was my father.

'Rose, please speak to me.'

Everything was so slow, and I had no words. Bathed in the light shining through the door was Tom Verger, carrying a sack and holding many parcels. There was a warm heaviness on my shoulders as he draped me in my soft quilt. I wrapped it around me and breathed in the scent of home. Lavender from the little sachets May used to tuck into my pillow to try and bring me sweet dreams. Tom Verger fetching me these gifts was more love than I could bear.

'There's some of your clothes as well and some clean straw for you. Oh, dear God.'

He knelt beside me and I could see that he was weeping. Why would a man weep at the notion of providing straw for his daughter?

'There's milk, some mutton and bread and cheese. Oh, Rose. Please speak so I know you're alive.'

'Tom,' I said at last. My tongue was thick. I was so very hot and yet I shivered.

'Thank God. Take some milk. Here. Careful, so it doesn't spill.'

The thought of milk spilling scared me because the new me would kneel down and lick it up.

'Your hands are trembling. Here, I'll open it for you. Can you hold it, Rose? Can you?'

I took the flask from him and my mouth filled with the creamy taste of our own herd. Tom had brought so many packages and flasks. There would be enough food for days if I could keep the vermin off it. While drinking, I began tucking the packages into my shift.

He'd also brought my old cloak and frocks and some stockings and mittens. And enough straw to make a bed, with a little left to spread at the opposite side to cover my waste. My cell was still cold and damp and filthy and rat-infested, but I was no longer on my own.

'Thank you, Tom. Thank you. But where are Granny and May?'

'The turnkey wouldn't allow them in. Reckoned it was no place for decent women. Sorry. What am I thinking of saying that to you? We've been here for days but they wouldn't allow any visitors till they had the proper dispensation from the archdeacon, on account of well, the charges...'

He meant they wouldn't let anyone in because I was a witch, just like my mother and grandmother before me, but he couldn't bring himself to say it.

'Anyway,' he went on. 'Bet told me to fetch these provisions to you and the turnkey's been paid to make sure you're properly cared for. Are you well, Rose? And how about the bairn? Is he moving?'

I felt my middle. 'He's not moving. More tears rolled down my face. 'He's not moved since they brought me here.'

'Don't cry, hinny. He'll be sleeping. That's all it is, I'm certain of it. Sleeping.'

'Will you stay with me?'

'The turnkey said I can stop for an hour or so.'

'Will you watch over me while I sleep, and will you come again?'

'I'll watch over you, and I'll come back as often as they'll let me. God bless you and keep you. Oh, Rose, I'd give anything to change places and spare you from this.'

Ignoring this rash pledge, I lay in my nest of straw, warmly clad in stockings, two frocks, mittens, boots and a cloak. Clutching Gyb in one hand, I drew my quilt over me with the other and wept with gratitude at having a full belly, a warm bed and people who loved me enough to provide for me in my hour of greatest need.

The Proving of Widow Leaton

PATIENCE

I occupied pride of place in the front row of the wood-panelled courtroom. Beside me, Father bowed his head, lips moving in prayer. The court brimmed with sergeants, constables and officers, along with parishioners from Mutton Clog, the cathedral men and numerous inquisitive strangers.

Whilst our journey to Durham had been fraught on account of the ice impeding our progress, it was pleasant being in the city amongst people of intellect and society for a change. And if today went according to plan, Father and I might soon be released from the purgatory of our current parish.

Finally, the sergeants went to fetch the witch from the gaol. Scarcely two months had elapsed since my accusation, but with each passing day I grew more weary with waiting. Nevertheless, her time had come and justice would be served at long last. When they dragged her in, a hush fell across the court as the sergeants bullied my sister-in-law into the dock.

In the two months since her arrest, the change in her gave me pause. Gaunt and filthy, she was all arms and legs, apart from her vast belly. Her cheekbones stuck out, and her eyes were too large and bright, as if she had succumbed to consumption. The jurymen filed into their box to the side of the elevated bench and once they were settled, a liveried official ordered us to rise. The clerk called the room to order and the justice entered. A mere spindle of a man, he slipped into his throne behind the bench, prim in his silver wig and black gown. Only when there was silence did he begin his preamble.

'This morning, we have cleared the calendar to hear the case of Widow Leaton from the parish of Mutton Clog. The charges are that she is both witch and consort of the devil.' He pinched the bridge of his nose and exhaled. 'However, we are modern men these days. Men of science. So we shall investigate these charges thoroughly and take nothing at face value.' He addressed my sister-in-law. 'What is your name?'

'Rose Leaton, née Driver.'

'And you are a widow, is that right?'

'Yes, your honour. My late husband died at sea while serving as a naval chaplain.'

'The son of your local priest, yes?'

'He was, yes.'

'Thank you, Widow Leaton. And the accuser is your sister-in-law?'

'I believe my late husband's sister has accused me, yes.'

He nodded. 'This is a delicate matter, but would you like to plead your belly and spare your child? I will allow it.'

Whose side was the justice on, with this flagrant misuse of justicial discretion? At the risk of being held in contempt, I objected.

'What my sister-in-law carries in her womb is no child and has a more demonic provenance. Please do not permit her to plead her belly, your honour, because she carries within her something quite unholy.'

On hearing this, the defendant's blood fled to her neck and cheeks, all but confessing her guilt.

'See how her face is florid with sin?' I pointed out. 'It is as good as a confession.'

'It's no confession,' she protested. 'I bear your brother's child.'

'Liar! The prisoner will claim anything to save her neck.'

'Settle yourself, Miss Leaton.' The justice waved me down. 'In all likelihood, your brother's widow bears his child. I must caution you that if you insist on pursuing your accusation, and your sister-in-law is put to death, then you kill alongside her your own flesh and blood, the living legacy of your late brother. Is that really what you hope to achieve here today?'

'Your honour, I hope only to ensure that you have all the necessary evidence. There can be no reprieve for this woman since her maternal grandmother was tried as a witch and executed.'

The accused did not take kindly to the sharing of this news and she fixed her gaze on me whilst addressing the bench.

'My grandmother's trial was a travesty, your honour. Everyone says so. She was no witch but an innocent citizen hanged on the say-so of a crazed man who loved money as much as he hated women.'

The justice rubbed his forehead as if trying to erase his wrinkles. 'Widow Leaton, you will not bandy about words like *travesty* in my courtroom. I offered you the opportunity to plead your belly, but in view of your pedigree, we must forgo that clemency and proceed. Your accuser has sworn a statement that you carry not her brother's child but something more unholy. While it strikes me as improbable, I will keep an open mind and hear the evidence.' He turned to the clerk at his side. 'Read out the first indictment.'

'Item one,' announced the clerk, 'Widow Leaton stands accused of attempting to procure a miscarriage.'

On hearing this, the commoners in the public gallery

guffawed and the witch lowered her head, covering her belly as best she could with her hands.

'For goodness' sake.' The justice leant over the clerk. 'Whose miscarriage was Widow Leaton procuring, exactly?'

'Her own, your honour.'

The justice considered her swollen form. 'Evidently, the Widow Leaton has failed in this regard – that is, if she even made such an attempt. Charges of this sort are notoriously difficult to prove. Had I been informed the widow was so obviously with child, this charge would never have been allowed. Dismissed. Strike it from the record, clerk. The birth looks imminent and I'd like to conclude this case before that eventuality. Read out the next charge.'

Red-faced, the clerk cleared his throat and made his announcement. 'Item two: unnatural practices concerning the products of birth and death.'

A murmur ran through the court at this and the justice expressed concern regarding the welfare of some members of the public.

'Is this evidence suitable for the ears of ladies? I note we have a number present.'

I interjected on their behalf. 'As a priest's daughter, if it is fit for me to say, I feel sure it is fit for other women to hear. We are not so very delicate as we are often portrayed.'

At this, the justice's eyes widened, but since no one made ready to leave, he allowed it.

'Continue, Miss Leaton, but be circumspect in your language and description, because I want no fainting in my courtroom.'

'Duly noted, your honour.' In the interests of impressing upon the justice and jury the veracity of my deposition, I consulted my journal before speaking. 'During the early days in my father's new parish I surprised the defendant at her work as a shepherdess. She flayed the skin from a lamb and thrust its remains into her bodice so it rested against her heart. Shortly afterwards, she took up another lamb, which looked dead to me and proceeded to cover it in the blood-stained pelt, fastening it on with witches' knots. O, I nearly swooned at the sight but she didn't so much as blink.' I shuddered at the memory. 'And judging by the deftness of her bladework, it was not her first outing with the flenching knife. Her hand was bloody where she'd cut it and allowed her own blood to commingle with that of the lamb she'd sacrificed to seal the pact with her dark master. And when I disturbed her in her gruesome work, she threatened my life.'

Following my evidence, there were several snorts from the crowd and the justice raised his hand for silence.

'And what do you think the defendant hoped to achieve with this grisly practice, Miss Leaton?' he asked.

'I cannot be certain because I fled in fear for my life and did not await the outcome of her ritual. But it is widely known that witches use the products of birth and death in their spell casting, and I am certain this was a spell used to raise a storm in order to kill me and ensnare my late brother as part of her hellish plan.'

From the tail of my eye, I observed Farmer Johnson get to his feet. The justice motioned him to sit down, but the insolent fellow remained standing.

'Do you wish to be imprisoned for contempt, man?'

'No, your honour. But with the greatest of respect, I do not want this Leaton lass to make a fool of the law, either.'

'The law is sufficiently robust to take care of itself, but if you must have your say, speak your name and declare any connection to the accused.'

'My name is Farmer Johnson – Will Johnson – and I am a long-standing friend of the Driver family. What the vicar's lass describes is everyday practice amongst shepherds. Not devilry at all but sound husbandry.' The justice raised his gavel but Johnson went on. 'This practice is something Rose's da taught her. Every farmer here's done it.' There came a chorus of grunts. 'It's the usual way when faced with a cade lamb, an orphan, that is. A shepherd will wrap the cade in the skin of a dead lamb to pass off the orphan to the bereft mother as her own offspring. It saves a lamb dying of hunger and a ewe dying of grief. Two lives saved with some skilful knifework.'

This practice still sounded magical to my ears, but the justice nodded along as if convinced.

'I'm not conversant with these traditions, Farmer Johnson, but your explanation does have the ring of truth about it.'

'That's because it is true. We all do it. Anyone with sheep has done it. Blenkinsop will tell you.'

His burly companion got up. 'Aye, it's true. There are other tricks for persuading a ewe to foster a cade lamb but I can promise you that method is definitely not fit for the ladies' ears.'

A few sniggers broke out until the justice barked over them.

'Pray, keep your cruder sheep-husbanding practices to yourself, Mr Blenkinsop. Sit down.'

The man flushed to the tips of his ears, but did as he was told. The justice jerked his chin at the clerk.

'Strike all remarks relating to lamb-rearing from the record. It seems this peculiar act constitutes a necessary part of shepherding, however questionable it may be for a woman to carry out such work.'

'But you did not see how she wielded the knife, your honour,' I argued. 'No woman should be that skilled in butchery. It is unnatural.'

Farmer Johnson remained standing, silently eyeing the justice as if finding him wanting. 'It's an ancient craft, shepherding,' said Johnson, 'carried out since the dawn of time. If a young lass can be hanged for tending her flock, then there's no hope for any of us.'

The justice sighed and ran a finger across the clerk's notes. 'Strike it all out. That includes any mention of knifework.' He addressed the jury. 'Ignore all that has been said so far. Evidently, the accused is a skilled shepherdess and these practices are part and parcel of that work. What Miss Leaton has described today may have been used to condemn women as witches in the past. Happily, we no longer hang innocents on the say-so of the local scolds, just as we no longer trust men with doctored pricking devices to test them.' He peered at me. 'While the Widow Leaton's garb is less than exemplary and she finds herself in a certain condition, I must ask myself whether this is a simple instance of a plain maid being jealous of another who is not-so-very plain?'

The justice's bid at humiliation did not deter me. 'I am as plain as a turnip, certainly, but I am a dedicated Christian and above the sin of envy. My concern is purely with the spiritual welfare of my father's parishioners, and it is neither fair nor reasonable to suggest I might be so wicked as to send a young woman to the gallows for possessing a bonnier face than that granted to me by God.'

The justice purpled, evidently not used to young women speaking back to him, and he did not like it. It would not do for me to get on his wrong side though, so I would refrain from badgering him, unless absolutely essential.

'I see we have a long list of indictments ahead of us,' said the justice. 'I am minded to hear only one more item, Miss Leaton, but must warn you that I am almost out of temper.'

'Your honour, I was saving the most heinous charge until last, but it is the most important of all so I choose that one. Please ask your clerk to read out the final indictment. Our very souls depend on it.'

'Very well. Clerk, as we are here, proceed with the final item.'

'Item three,' said the clerk, importantly. 'Non-observance of the sabbath for some twenty years, due to the Widow Leaton's inability to enter a church.'

'Non-observance is a serious matter, but I daresay there are plenty in this room who set foot more often in their local hostelry than their parish church. That said, if the defendant does not observe the sabbath because she is not able to enter church, it does warrant further investigation. Even so, I remain to be persuaded that this stands up to either a charge of witchcraft or of consorting with the devil.'

My case was in danger of crumbling, so I needed to buttress it.

'Your honour,' I said. 'This indictment can be proven simply by taking Widow Leaton into church. Her reaction will prove to you beyond any doubt that she is a witch, a woman in league with Satan. Please do it and you will see the truthfulness of my testament.' The justice was not convinced and this was my last chance so I consulted my journal once again, tapping my finger on the appropriate entry. 'On admission to the church on All Hallows' Eve, my sister-in-law screeched and thrashed, clawing at the eyes of any Christian who tried to help her. If that is not the sign of demonic infestation, I do not know what is.'

'And you have seen this behaviour manifest itself, have you, Miss Leaton?'

'Indeed, I saw it with my own eyes, as did my father, the parish priest, when we tested her ourselves, and I noted the results in this journal.' Now I had his interest. I twisted around and pointed at our sexton. 'Her natural father also witnessed it as he interrupted our holy work prior to carrying her away.'

'Her natural father? Oh, yes. I see they have the same colouring. Even so, we cannot afford to get distracted by that when we already have plenty to contend with this morning. On the face of it, the defendant's reaction does strike me as sinister, but before proceeding any further in this matter, I must invite representations on her behalf. Who will speak up for Rose Leaton?'

To my chagrin, every person from the valley stood up, apart from Father and our servant. Both Driver women stood up, along with Verger, Johnson, Blenkinsop and the three Green brothers. I would take these rogue parishioners to task next Sunday. The justice beckoned Thomas Verger.

'You there. The father. We have yet to hear from you. Tell us who you are.'

'Thomas Verger, sexton and warden for Mutton Clog parish. And I'm Widow Leaton's natural father.'

'Evidently not a particularly obedient or worthy warden if you have a natural daughter and announce it in open court without so much as a blush. Still, you're not on trial here, so proceed, Mr Verger. Tell me, did you witness this spectacle?'

'I did witness it, aye.' The sexton gave me a long look and breathed out slowly. 'It wasn't the first time I've seen me daughter suffer in this fashion. Twice now it's happened. The first time was at Easter when she was a bit bairn, but I wouldn't describe it as a spectacle. Just the torment of a little mite recently bereaved of her mother and infant brother.'

The justice ran a finger down the papers and the clerk made some notes. 'And after that Easter visit, did none of you think to take her to church again when she was older?'

'Your honour,' said Verger, 'after seeing her terror, no decent person would put anyone through such an experience twice, let alone a bairn.'

The justice held up his gavel to prevent the sexton from going on. Good. Hopefully, he would not accord too much credence to Verger since he shared blood with the defendant.

'Thank you, Mr Verger, that is all. On paper, these charges did appear to indicate witchcraft. However, after a measure of questioning, they have not held up.' He peered down from the bench at me. 'I am forced to conclude, Miss Leaton, that these accusations are spurious at the—' He waited to allow a couple of sergeants to settle the excitable elements who had flared up on learning they were to be deprived of seeing a witch executed.

It was unconscionable that Rose Driver would be

reprieved, whereas Father and I would be trapped at Mutton Clog for the rest of his days. I could not bear to remain in that country manse a second longer and had to try once more to redeem us.

'Please, your honour, if you release the defendant, you risk unleashing an evil entity on an otherwise innocent parish, and my father alone is not powerful enough to contain it. We need your help and the full weight of the law brought to bear. The slippery Mr Verger spoke of his natural daughter's childhood ordeal to gain the court's sympathy instead of answering your question and describing what he witnessed more recently.' I ignored the justice opening his mouth to speak and barrelled on whilst the floor was mine. 'A repeat of the test may cause my sister-in-law undue stress, but we have no proper explanation as to why that is. I posit that it is because the devil resides in her and in her child. No parishioner will be safe unless both are destroyed.' Next to me, my father groaned deeply, but I was in a passion and continued. 'I implore you to reveal the truth, your honour. Churching will cost you nothing but time, and where is the harm in that?'

The public gallery fell silent at the prospect of going to the cathedral to watch such an ordeal and would no doubt riot if deprived of it. When the justice closed his eyes in defeat, it was an effort for me to retain a suitably grave expression.

'The defendant's inability to enter church does concern me, somewhat,' he said at length before turning to address her. 'It will be easily disproved, my dear. It is one of the oldest tests for proving witchcraft. Ordeal by church.' He waved to the sergeants. 'Speak to the archdeacon, and arrange for this woman to be prostrated at the cathedral's high altar. If she can manage it in a normal fashion, she will be free to go, and if not, I must deliberate on the possibility that she is indeed guilty of witchcraft and of consorting with the devil.'

At these words, all the blood drained from the witch's face, the fire died in her eyes and even her lips were white. I looked down to hide my smile and thought back to Father's efforts to church her. Anyone witnessing that phenomenon could be left in no doubt as to the possession of my sister-in-law's soul.

The Truth Will Out

ROSE

This might be my only chance of survival. To withstand the ordeal without reacting as I had when entering church the last two times. Otherwise, with Patience salting the soup, I'd almost certainly hang and all because of the accusations of a bitter lass. How galling that so many people believed her ridiculous charges. A girl with far too much time on her hands, with naught to do but read, and naught to read but biblical texts. No wonder she was so warped. I doubted devils existed, but wouldn't share this opinion in court because denying the existence of Satan was akin to denying the existence of God, so I kept my peace.

Being forced inside the church a couple of months ago had shifted something in my head, flooding it with memories. And the memory of what I'd experienced that Candlemas as a bairn shrivelled my heart. But now I was armed with an understanding of the cause of my terror, it might help me to overcome it. Witnessing my mother's murder at such a tender age must have caused my mind to shut down. But although the memory was trapped behind a grey mass in my head, part of me had always remembered that horrific scene, and my nightmares and my strange game were an attempt to release me from it. Crossing the church threshold on All Hallows' Eve had unleashed so many memories, and since remembering, my dread had eased. After the grey mass faded away, I could see the past all too clearly. Now I might be able to enter the church like anyone else and had to try because my life and my child's life depended on it.

While the justice and the clerk were in discussion, Tom Verger stood up and smoothed his jerkin. What was he up to? Perhaps he would beg them not to church me again. But he'd no need because I could almost certainly endure the coming ordeal. The clerk noticed him and respectfully tapped the justice's shoulder so he looked up.

'What is it, Mr Verger?'

'Please, your honour,' said Tom. 'I can explain Widow Leaton's reaction. If you will hear me out, it might spare her from the ordeal.'

Patience Leaton held up her hand. 'Your honour, I beg you, are we all to sit here whilst this man fills our ears with his repulsive lies?'

'I will permit him to speak, Miss Leaton. You have had your say – and how – so he will have his. Go ahead, Verger.

'Thank you, your honour. There is a sound reason why my daughter cannot set foot in church and it has naught to do with any devil, at least not any devil from hell.'

Did Tom think he could help me? Patience seemed to think so and rose from her chair, puffed up with indignation and ready for a new attack, but the justice refused to hear her out.

'Miss Leaton, kindly remain seated, while we hear from Mr Verger.'

'If possible, your honour,' said Tom, 'can I ask that my daughter is removed from the court? She should not have to hear what I have to say. Not in her condition.'

This request was weighed for a few moments but the justice refused. 'Widow Leaton is material to the case and must remain here.'

Why did Tom want me removed when I already knew what he was about to say about my mother's murder?

He glanced at me and started to speak. 'I need to go back twenty-odd years,' he said. 'You might recall the Newcastle witch trials almost quarter of a century ago, when the common council there fetched down a Scottish witchfinder, John Sharpe?'

'He is known to me, yes,' said the justice. 'I believe he escaped to Scotland?'

'He did, aye, but he returned to England and fetched up at our parish the following Candlemas, when Widow Leaton was a bairn.'

My knees turned to water as the awful retelling began, and the clerk left the bench and guided me to a seat. I took a steadying breath to prepare myself and the courtroom fell silent as Tom reported how the witchfinder ripped my brother from the womb and murdered him. How Tom arrived too late and my mother died in his arms. How, unknown to anyone, I'd witnessed their murders. Through my tears, I saw for the first time his pain and how much he loved my mother

He'd buried my mother and brother in the graveyard and let it be known that they'd died in childbed. Could he ever know the damage he'd caused with this lie – even if it was well meant – and that I'd nearly destroyed my baby for fear of following my mother into an early grave? But it was unfair to hold it against him when he'd tried so hard to help my mother, my brother and me, and now he was here, speaking up for me and risking his own neck.

'As a sexton,' said the justice, 'you are aware that you should have reported these murders to the coroner?'

'Aye, your honour, I'm aware of it and will take whatever punishment is due to me, but for the sake of me daughter, I cannot stay silent any more.'

The justice consulted the clerk, who in turn consulted a large book. I wondered what punishment Tom would get for his admission, and whether they would sentence him straight away or put him in gaol till they found a date on the calendar.

'We will address the matter of your failure to report two murders in due course, but I have some further questions in the interim. After you witnessed these murders, what happened to Sharpe? Where was the witchfinder in all this?'

'Lurking in the church shadows,' said Tom. 'He never left.'

'If your tale bears water, then you have adequately explained why Widow Leaton is unable to enter a church, but you will appreciate that I cannot take you at your word, especially as you are the natural father of the accused. Where is this John Sharpe villain now?'

I willed Tom to stay quiet. The very last thing I wanted was for him to sacrifice himself for me, but he kept going.

'I burnt the witchfinder on a pyre, your honour. Alive.'

At this revelation, the courtroom erupted till the sergeants restored order.

'Alive, Verger? You burnt the man alive?'

'Aye, I did, because John Sharpe lived and breathed only to torture and slay women so I made sure he'd slay no more.'

I couldn't believe that Tom was capable of murder, even of a man as wicked as John Sharpe, or that he'd freely admitted it in court. He would hang for it.

'Mr Verger,' said the justice. 'Do you consider it wise to confess to such a grave crime, without first seeking counsel? I cannot consider an application for benefit of clergy due to the serious nature of this felony, but you may wish to seek another form of amelioration.'

'My confession stands. I need no advice, your honour.'

'Ill advised, Mr Verger, ill advised, but you are your own man. Where are Sharpe's remains?'

'Scattered to the four winds, so he'd have no final resting place.'

'How convenient. We have a woman and her child

murdered, assumed dead of childbirth, and a man that no one has ever missed, allegedly killed by you, with no remains to prove his presence.' The justice cupped his chin while he conferred with the clerk before resuming his interrogation. 'And you are this woman's father and hope to ease her punishment by taking it on your own shoulders. I suppose it is laudable in some regards. Not many men would sacrifice themselves on behalf of a child, least of all a daughter, and a natural one at that. But this tale of yours does not ring true. I fear you are trying to corrupt the course of justice to benefit Widow Leaton. Few could blame you for this, but I cannot allow it to pass, so we must proceed with the ordeal–'

A small fuss broke out, and I saw May quarrelling and trying to stop Granny getting to her feet.

'The lad is telling the truth,' said Granny, swatting away May's hands and facing the justice.

'Tell me how you came by this knowledge, but first give your name and your connection to the accused.'

'I am Elizabeth Driver. Widow Leaton is my granddaughter and my late son was her legitimate father.'

'Well, this is without precedent in my court. While many defendants have no father to speak of, it's something of a first to find one with two.'

Granny raised her chin, belligerent as ever and didn't falter. 'My son, Andrew Driver, married Rosie's mother before the bairn was born – before Rosie was born, I mean. And to answer your original question, I came by this knowledge because my late husband and son were also present at the burning of John Sharpe, along with Tom Verger's father, Bill, and Reverend Cuthbert Foster, may God rest all their souls.'

Granny told the court what Tom had told me in his shack on All Hallows' Eve. How Bill Verger roused the household in the dead of night, leaving me with her while he took Da and Granda with him, and what they reported on returning home. All the while, she wrung her hands, but she never once looked down.

'My menfolk told me of a sight they would wish on no man: our Jane and baby Jim murdered. When we'd retired earlier on, my grandson hadn't yet been born, and we weren't expecting him for a few months.' Granny swallowed noisily. 'Inside the church, Jim and Andrew couldn't see anything at first. But they could smell blood. So much so, the air was thick with the stench of it. And they knew it wasn't the blood of a beast – any farmer would know – and as they drew closer, they saw Verger blood-soaked. Then they saw them butchered.'

'And by *them* you refer to your grandson and your daughter-in-law?'

'Your honour,' Granny said, 'The child was named Jim, for my late husband, so please give my little grandson his name.'

The justice grimaced. 'Please accept my apologies, Widow Driver. He shall have his name. The infant, Jim Driver. Please go on.'

Granny told how Da and Granda found my baby brother slaughtered on the altar and my mother on the floor. Because Tom was covered in blood, at first Da and Granda supposed him guilty, till they noticed a stranger lashed to a pillar and also drenched in blood. Granny swayed slightly and swiped at her eyes as she told the court how Reverend Foster had identified him as the witchfinder, John Sharpe.

That man had held a deep grudge against my poor mother since she'd escaped the hangman's noose at the witch trials, and he'd travelled far and wide in search of her, determined to finish her and me. It was a terrible tale. Tom had told it to me on All Hallows' Eve after my churching. It seemed unreal then and it still seemed unreal now.

'And this must have enraged your son?' said the justice. 'I understand he was far from fight-shy?'

Granny swallowed. 'It was always our Andrew's way to

protect his family, your honour.' She stared at a spot past the justice's head before coming to. 'But the shock of what he'd seen did something to my lad. He was no stranger to death and butchery. No farmer is. Our work demands it and that work hardens you. But this...' Her face blanched at the memory. 'The five of them did it together. Five men. My son and husband, Tom Verger and his father, Bill, and Reverend Foster. Together, the men of Mutton Clog put John Sharpe to death. They executed him to save Rosie. Only one of them is left alive today, but here he is, bless him, ready to save her again.'

Granny's evidence supported Tom's version of events, but it sealed his fate, and perhaps her own. Although she'd taken no part in any killing, she'd known about it and the justice could punish her, though I doubted she'd hang for it. I did fear for what these confessions meant for Tom. My natural father had laid down his life and would be taken from this world. All because of one vindictive girl.

Patience Leaton's complexion was crimson with all the excitement of the day and her chest rose and fell as she panted for breath. In the months she'd lived in our parish, I'd never seen the lass possess such high colour. She was having her day with us. I hoped a good man's life was worth it for her.

The Longest Night
PATIENCE

What an astonishing reversal of fortune. I had been intent on punishing my sister-in-law, but faced with the prospect of her execution, Thomas Verger broke his twenty-year silence and sacrificed himself to save his natural daughter. Whilst I had failed in my original mission, this was still an acceptable outcome as that vile woman would spend the remainder of her days with his death weighing on her conscience.

During Verger's initial statement, I despaired. His explanation as to why his daughter could not enter church sounded all too plausible and I feared she would walk free. But I could not have dreamt of what he later admitted, corroborated by Elizabeth Driver. He did not hesitate. Neither did he hide behind words to excuse himself. And the justice wasted no time in picking over the bones of his story.

Perhaps most shocking of all, Verger bore responsibility for this whole chain of events. Our apparently wholesome sexton had connived to flee with Andrew Driver's pregnant goodwife and their daughter, planning to sail to the New World. Which is why she was hiding in the church on that Candlemas night. Had Thomas Verger not attempted to take to the high seas with another man's goodwife, the woman would have been at home in bed like a good Christian and would most likely still be alive today, having raised her son and daughter and a few more siblings besides.

§

The court session had left me wrung out. Mercifully, the justice ordered a short recess, and the clerk instructed everyone but my sister-in-law and her two protectors to leave and find refreshment, with the three of them to be held in custody.

Replete, we now resumed our places in court once more and rose when the clerk instructed us. The justice entered, took his seat and opened the session.

'On balance, I consider that Widow Leaton has been the victim of a vicious campaign coordinated by her sister-in-law, Patience Leaton. Where is she? Ah, there you are. Come here. Yes, you.'

I stood before him and tried to meet his eye.

'I can think of no good reason for your motive, Miss Leaton, but you initiated this spiteful attack for your own amusement, and you nearly sent an innocent woman and her unborn child to the gallows. An act of grievous mischief. I am a great believer in letting the punishment fit the crime. Should you so much as whisper another false allegation, I will have you transported and you can see how they like your wiles in the New World. Providing you do not appear before me again, I am prepared to accept that your twin brother's death at sea unbalanced your mind. My condolences to you and Minister Leaton. Now sit down.'

My face burned. How dare he question my motives and sanity? And as for threatening to send me to the New World! Father slipped his right arm around my shoulders and took both my hands in his left. Not for comfort but restraint. The indignity almost brought me to tears in a public place, but I controlled myself. An ability my sister-in-law would do well to learn. Her dirty face was streaked with tearstains and she made no effort to clean herself up. In soft tones, the justice invited her to remain seated.

'Widow Leaton, you are exonerated from all charges.' The justice rapped the sounding block with his gavel. 'This case is dismissed.' He leant over to my sister-in-law and addressed her. 'You are free to go my dear, and I am sorry for all you have endured in recent weeks. Go to your people. Go on.'

I watched the dazed woman as she hobbled forwards. In her position, I would have run from the court before the verdict was reversed. Her family and neighbours closed around her, talking all at once, until the justice raised his voice.

'Before you forget yourselves and start to celebrate, let me remind you that serious charges remain to be addressed. I cannot turn a blind eye to what amounts to cold-blooded murder by Thomas Verger and four other men. Neither can I ignore the fact that Elizabeth Driver knew of this wrong-doing and kept the knowledge to herself all these years. Given the serious nature of this case, we will recess for three hours while I consider the evidence. Clerk, clear the calendar for this afternoon. I will hear their pleas, such as they are, and determine sentence. Thomas Verger and Elizabeth Driver will remain in the custody of the court.'

&

Even though it was Advent and we should be fasting, Father insisted on taking me to a nearby chophouse for our midday meal. He counselled me not to return to court, especially considering the explicit threat of transportation. However, I decided not to heed his advice. Having come this far, I needed to hear the final verdict.

Whilst Father refrained from eating, I replenished my strength and forced down a plateful of lamb cutlets and a dish of bread pudding. Later, one of the archdeacon's men approached our table. He did not address me, but leant close to my father to drop a message in his ear before leaving. But I heard every word. Like so many people in their sixth decade, the man's ears were failing and so he spoke loudly to compensate, all the while believing himself discreet.

The justice was in no hurry to appear in the courtroom and I imagined him lingering over his midday repast. Almost an hour later, he entered, looking irritable and worn out rather than replete. The clerk ordered everyone to sit, apart from the two accused. The justice probed his molars with his tongue, wincing slightly before beginning.

'Thomas Verger, you have confessed to a serious crime. Four men have escaped without penalty for their part in the murder, and so we must pray that a higher power has punished them. You, in particular, as an employee of the church and an elected official, must know better than most that murder is both a sin and a crime.'

The two prisoners, despite having a good deal to be ashamed of, did not hang their heads.

'I won't apologise for what I did,' said the sexton, 'not to you and not to God. If we'd handed Sharpe to the sergeants, he'd have slipped his bounds as he did in Newcastle and yet again in Berwick.'

'Aye,' added Elizabeth Driver, unabashed. 'My son and husband wanted to go to their grave, secure in the knowledge that Sharpe couldn't harm our Rosie, so she'd grow up free of this evil shadow hanging over her. For make no mistake, sire, the witchfinder wouldn't have rested till he'd butchered her and all. He had to die. There was no other way.'

'I must beg to differ,' said the justice. 'Widow Driver,

while you cannot be held responsible for what took place that night, you should have done your duty and informed the proper authorities and let justice take its course. Instead, you kept this knowledge to yourself. This is a serious offence, but granted, less serious than murder. In view of your advanced years, and because you were placed in this invidious position through no fault of your own, I am prepared to show a degree of mercy.'

The old woman sagged in relief. How irksome that she would escape with a mere reprimand.

'Elizabeth Driver, for your part in covering up the unlawful death of John Sharpe, however unwitting, you will forfeit your tenancy and everything you own. Your livestock, your crops and stores, all your possessions and savings. You may keep what you stand up in and no more. Approach the clerk for instruction.'

Despite her weather-beaten complexion, upon hearing this sentence, Elizabeth Driver paled as she realised the consequences of leaping to her granddaughter's defence. She had aged a decade since this morning, leaving her resembling the elderly widow she was. Her fellow convict, on the other hand, was as vital as ever, drawing strength from the act of saving his daughter. It was a small consolation to me that the three Driver women would live out their days in penury.

Once Elizabeth Driver had been dealt with by the clerk and embraced by her family, the justice went on.

'Thomas Verger, you have belatedly confessed to the murder of John Sharpe. Not content with killing him, you deprived him of a Christian burial. Taking the law into your own hands in this way might appeal to many as a fair solution but you remain subject to the law, no matter what has been done to you or your loved ones. While I have some sympathy with your cause, at day's end you murdered an official employed on council business, then acted in concert to cover up your handiwork.'

He took stock of the prisoner, who did not lower his chin. Thomas Verger would be rightly rewarded for his sinful lack of humility.

'Murder is crime enough, but conspiring to kill an official in the course of his authorised work compounds the error.' The justice held up a hand to stifle any objection. 'I am left with no choice, therefore, but to make an example of you.' The justice rifled in a drawer and withdrew a small cap of black silk, which he placed with all due reverence over his wig.

'Thomas Verger, for the part you played in the conspiracy to murder John Sharpe, you will be taken at break of day to the gallows and hanged by the neck until you are dead. May God have mercy on you.'

My sister-in-law looked sick at these tidings. Unable to compose herself, she had to be restrained by Blenkinsop to prevent her from running at me. Perturbed by Rose Driver's attempted assault, Father ushered me towards the door. Our path was blocked, however, by members of the public gallery surging into the late-afternoon streets before filing into chophouses and inns to celebrate or commiserate. We had no choice but to wait for the courtroom to empty whilst our parishioners' eyes blazed with hatred.

'Perhaps it would be wise for you to dine in your chamber at the inn. I shall ask the keeper's wife to arrange it. Otherwise, make sure your door stays locked. I will go to the gaol and keep vigil with our sexton if he will permit me to pray with him. It is the very least I can do for the man.'

'This outcome is not the result I wanted, Father, far from it, but the discovery of a murdered witchfinder and the seizure of such a prosperous farm have boded well with the archdeacon. You must be pleased that you will be reinstated in your former post come Easter.'

Father grasped me by my shoulders. 'Yes, but at what cost, Patience? At what cost?'

‌‌

As night descended, I shivered as if it were entering my soul and was relieved to reach the warmth and light of the inn. I intended to retire early to insure against oversleeping and missing the hanging. Father counselled me against attending, but nothing would deter me from reaping the reward of my labours. and so he left me and walked to the gaol, giving up his sleep to keep vigil.

Verger had sacrificed himself for my worthless sister-in-law and deserved to die. In breaking the sixth commandment, he had murdered a witchfinder, who would have gone on to discover many more witches. John Sharpe's career was halted prematurely, and it grieved me to think of all the evil he might have prevented in the world had he been allowed to live out his natural life. Because he had been killed decades before his time, countless hags were left free to continue their foul practices, my sister-in-law amongst them.

Whilst my attempt to prosecute a witch had resulted in failure yet again, I had successfully prosecuted a man whose actions had indirectly permitted many witches to go free. Regrettably, his four conspirators had escaped their earthly retribution, but I trusted God would punish them according to their sins. Verger would die for what he had done and that would have to suffice.

‌‌

It was here. The shortest day of the year, when England would barely see light before returning again to darkness. Happily, I woke long before dawn, dressed and hurried outside. Father had not returned to the inn, so I set out for the hanging fields alone. They were not difficult to find, as the streets massed with people filing out of the heart of the city. The cobbles underfoot were treacherous with ice, forcing me to walk slowly and watch where I put my feet. Although submerged in the anonymous grey throng of crass entertainment seekers, I felt God's eye was on me. He knew that this hanging was on my account, and I was not anonymous to Him. The knowledge warmed me on this, the coldest of mornings.

As we reached the site, the sky lost some of its grey. A faint light showed itself in the east, washing the horizon in a watery yellow. The onlookers were jammed shoulder to shoulder and I had to push myself through the bloodthirsty assembly.

The outline of the gallows emerged. At its foot knelt my father alongside Verger, both their heads bowed in prayer. Why would any priest waste his good breath on a futile endeavour to bring this lost lamb to God? Close by, the two Widows Driver comforted my sister-in-law, agony etched on all three of their simple peasant faces. They lacked basic decency, crying for themselves, which would be of little comfort to a man about to die.

Above us, the sky gradually lit up with glorious red fire. A warning sky. When my father finished praying, he got to his feet, the prisoner with him, and my shameless sister-in-law cried out, hands cradling her belly.

'Tom Verger, your grandson will be named Joseph Thomas James Leaton.'

On hearing this, he smiled and I wondered at his vanity, that he might think a child of his blood carrying his name would somehow let him live on. And what a ridiculous number of names for a child, as if he were a king in the making. Of course, no one but me stopped to wonder how the witch knew she would give birth to a boy.

Quite apart from her sinful prognostication, she had delivered a final insult to my family. The list of names proposed for this infant was so long as to be vulgar, yet my brother's Christian name was omitted. It was a slight both cruel and short-sighted.

Having now learnt about the goings on at Mutton Clog over two decades ago, Father had vacillated once again. No longer did he believe his daughter-in-law to be a witch and he was convinced again that her child was my brother's son. But this omission in nomenclature would hurt him, and he might be dissuaded from having anything more to do with her. She would have nothing and no one. Weak from her incarceration, with no farm to sustain her, she might wither and die, and her infant with her.

Perhaps, now that she had fallen on hard times, we could remove the child and name him Hector Earnest Leaton. Our servant would be more than capable of raising him. But the unborn infant could wait and I turned my attention to the condemned man and the gallows that would terminate his life.

The executioner stood behind his captive and placed the noose around his neck, adjusting the knot for tightness and position. The stubborn prisoner refused a hood, stupidly choosing to look at his daughter for every last second. A fool to the end.

The noisy crowd hushed. A drum began to beat as Thomas Verger climbed the ladder. When he reached the top rung, the drumbeat palled, and the only sound came from the oblivious birds, singing as the sun rose higher. As one, the crowd began to jeer. Deservedly so. Nobody deserved public disdain more than a church official in disgrace. I hoped his death would be a drawn-out affair, since he had been the primary reason my sister-in-law did not receive her just deserts.

Verger balanced atop the ladder that would deliver him on his final journey, a black silhouette against a red sky, fists clenched at his sides, waiting for the jeers of the crowd to die down before speaking. His last words were not to beg the Lord for forgiveness but wasted on that worthless woman. He called out to his natural daughter as joyfully as if he were about to embark on a pleasure jaunt.

'God grant you a long life, Rose. To you and to your son, Joseph. Do not be sad for me. I pray you both goodness and strength and health. I want my last sight on this earth to be you, my much-loved daughter. Then I go at last to my lovely Jane. Me and your mother will watch over you together.'

He would be in for a shock on reaching heaven, assuming he was permitted entry, because this *lovely Jane* would not be waiting for him. She would already be reunited with her legitimate husband, Andrew Driver. That thought cheered me greatly.

When they shoved Verger from the ladder, my sister-in-law wept without shame. For all his height and breadth, his neck did not break, and he strangled, large feet kicking as his whole body flailed. If he had hoped to exit this life in a dignified manner, then he had failed magnificently in that regard, and he looked likely to swing for some time.

Disappointingly, my own father turned traitor once again. He took a running jump at Thomas Verger and seized his feet, and by adding his own weight, thereby helped his former sexton into the next world.

SPRING

Meg Wetherby's Cottage

ROSE

These past months, Granny had been lost in her own private storm, alternately raging at the loss of her widow-right and weeping for the loss of her son. But when May lifted my baby from me and began rubbing him vigorously in the twilight, Granny gave over raging and weeping long enough to cast an eye over him.

'Dear God,' she said. 'That child is the living image of Tom Verger. Oh, it would have killed our Andrew. It's like the day you were born, Rosie. I wanted to put a bonnet on you to cover all that red hair.'

Silence worked best with Granny when she was on her high horse. May settled the baby on my collapsed belly and I nursed my beautiful child. My grandmother was right though, and while Joseph had the Leaton name, that's all he'd inherited from that family. His blood and colouring made him very much a Verger.

I tucked my blanket around him and latched him onto my left breast, smoothing his cheek with my pinkie to encourage him to suckle. I stroked the soft, red down on my son's head as he snuffled at my teat, his lovely green eyes fluttering. Hearing Granny working herself up into a state would be bad for the bairn, so I sang softly to him, hoping that he'd hear only me and my song.

Of course, I understood my grandmother's fury. She'd lost all her family, everything she'd ever owned and all that she'd worked for. It must hurt her seeing me and my child with our lives ahead of us while she neared the end of hers.

The court lost no time in seizing the tenancy and sold all the stock at auction. Farmer Johnson bought Barebones for me, and no one at the mart bid against him. We were three widows and a collie with nowhere to live so we'd moved into Meg Wetherby's cottage. However humble, we lived safely here, warm and dry. I said a silent thank you to Tom for looking after it for all these years.

I couldn't allow myself the luxury of tears about the events of recent months because Joseph had to come first. He would be my comfort and light. I marvelled at his delicate fingers furled around one of mine. His puckered face made him look cross at being called into the world too soon, but as the minutes went by, his face unpuckered and he yawned and stretched, his red lips murmuring soundlessly, glistening with milk.

When May hovered over me with a bowl of pottage, my belly growled. I'd not felt this famished since gaol. Reluctantly, I exchanged my baby for the bowl and wolfed down the pottage while my stepmother swaddled my child and rocked him. She would be a lovely granny. I thought of all she'd given up in life. Being a widow brought with it freedom, and hopefully a better life to come.

'Come on, up you get, Rose. Bet's asleep so while there's peace, why not get yourself cleaned up and changed? Farmer Johnson has given us his late wife's shifts, and some sheets to cut into rags.'

While May busied herself with the baby, I dipped rags into boiled water and cleaned myself, applying some dry rags to help staunch the bleeding.

'You'll bleed for a moon or two,' she said, smiling at

Joseph, dandling him in the air before sniffing his tiny backside.

'The little one is ready for a clean, too, by the smell of him,' she said, wrinkling her nose. 'At least all his innards are in fine working order.'

A bit more comfortable, I reached for him. May would have cleaned and changed him for me, but I preferred to do it myself. Since he'd arrived, I didn't want to imagine a minute without holding him. He was such a small scrap and for a second I recalled my brother and his birth. But no more than a second. I wouldn't let the darkness in. I needed to be strong and wouldn't raise my bairn in the shadow of all the deaths that preceded him.

Once clean, Joseph mewled and my breasts ached as my milk started coming in, so I drew him to me again.

'Bet's having herself a canny sleep, mind,' said May.

Just as well. She was almost as cross with my stepmother as she was with me. Farmer Johnson had asked May to keep house for him, and had promised her a gold ring for her finger once summer solstice came and went. The kindly farmer was close to twice her age, so hopefully she'd be able to put aside her decoctions and herbs and live a happy life at long last.

Barebones whimpered and lay down next to my grandmother's feet. Poor lass, she'd been left to her own devices for hours now.

'Give Granny a nudge, please, May. If she wakes up in a chair in the morning, she'll be stiff and it'll hardly improve her temper.'

May got up and patted Granny's cheek softly but she didn't stir. At once, I saw the pallor. So, my grandmother had gone, with only a few weeks of winter left. It didn't surprise me, really. Her heart broke when she lost Da and again after forfeiting the farm and all her memories. I wished her peace.

'If you'll take the bairn, I'll get up and lay her out.'

Granny had tended to me all my life, and now I'd tend to her.

'You'll stay exactly where you are, Rose. I'll see to Bet. I'll ask our Henry to collect her as fast as he can because she'll start lifting soon and you don't want that, not with a new baby in the house.'

The archdeacon had asked Henry Green to step in as sexton, and I felt sure Tom would have approved.

'I've some coins hidden away. Give one to your Henry to pay for Granny's burial. Put your hand behind those crocks on the top shelf. There's a small wooden box. They're in there.'

May stood on the cracket and reached up to pull out the box. It contained six coins, the golden angels Tom had sent across the sea to my mother when she was carrying me. Only, she'd never spent them and gave them to Bill Verger. When his father died, Tom passed the coins to Farmer Johnson for safekeeping, and asked him to hold them for me. From beyond the grave, my parents would provide for me and Joseph.

'Rose, where did you find this box?'

'Just there. I found it back when me, Tilly and Henry used to play in here.'

'What was inside when you found it?'

It had been a long time ago when we played our secret game, but I did recall an odd thing in there.

'A scrap of wax,' I said, 'or lambskin or some such,'

She looked at me queerly. 'What happened to it?'

'I threw it away, I think. No, wait. I burnt it on the fire, right here. Why do you ask?'

'It held Tom Verger's caul. Meg Wetherby kept it here and Tom always reckoned it's what stopped him drowning at sea aboard *The Durham*.'

A thought struck me. 'May, Tom didn't die because I burnt his caul.'

My stepmother looked at me oddly. 'I didn't say that,

Rose, or even think it.' She put her hand over her mouth as if deciding whether or not to speak her mind.

'Go on, May. Whatever it is, you might as well say it.'

'You know, the mart wives say that a man born to be hanged can never drown.'

Her words were like a slap in the face and sent me reeling back to that cruel day. Immediately, I forced it from my mind. I wouldn't waste Tom Verger's precious sacrifice by getting mired in the sorrow and superstitions of yesteryear and I had to stop my stepmother pulling me back.

'Oh, May. You can't really believe in those old sayings? The mart wives make them up to suit themselves. Haven't you noticed, they always mutter their wise saws after the event and not before?'

I reached down to rub the dog's ears and smiled to soften my words but my stepmother didn't return my smile. May wasn't much older than me, but she clung to the old beliefs.

'I never took you for superstitious,' I said. 'Tom not drowning was luck and naught more. And as for his...' The word *caul* died in my mouth. No man was born to hang. I refused to believe it.

She replaced the golden angels in the box and put it back on the shelf.

'Don't worry yourself, Rose. Our Henry will bury your granny as a favour. Bet Driver was a godsend to me, and to Tilly, and she was good to our Henry and all.'

She lowered her eyes whenever she mentioned her sister. After all that had happened, I'd scarcely thought of Tilly and what she'd done. She'd been my friend once, like a sister even. For all those years, she and her brother had played that nightmarish game with me.

Little had we known, but the innocent act of withdrawing my poppet from beneath Tilly's pinny was me reliving my brother's birth. Seeing him have his throat cut, again and again and again was me reliving my brother's death. And running the witchfinder through with a stick, was me childishly trying to change the past.

Back then, none of us knew what we were about. Now, I knew and so must Henry and Tilly. And so must May, since she'd walked in on our game. Although no one had ever said a word to me, all four of us now knew I'd made my childhood friends relive the butchering of my mother and brother in my unwitting attempt to redeem the past by killing the man who'd murdered them. It was so very long ago when we were innocent children, and I'd had no notion of where this game had originated, but still...

Tilly had been close to me once, but she'd betrayed me and thrown in her lot with the Leatons, and so best of luck to her. She'd not even tried to make amends, but Minister Leaton had. He'd struggled through the woods to the cottage, bearing my mother's satchel, still filled with the baby clothes knitted by her.

'I cannot make up for the misery my family has caused yours,' he said. 'And I cannot undo that pain. I will punish myself by never allowing myself to set eyes on my grandson, and will love him from afar, for my influence has unleashed something uncanny in my daughter. I fear for anyone who crosses her. The fault lies with me for letting her have her head. You will not see us again for we are returning to Ely to my former living. I have written to the Church and to the Navy to petition them so that you might have a widow's pension. I leave you with my blessings and this satchel.'

I couldn't look at him without seeing Earnest and Patience and all they'd taken from me, so I was pleased he was leaving.

'I will not take your blessing, Minister Leaton, but I will take what is rightfully mine.' I seized the satchel. 'And as you travel home, think on that you Leatons have bought your way out of Mutton Clog with the blood of a good man.'

❧

After laying Granny Driver to rest beside her husband, her son and her daughter, May moved in with Farmer Johnson, and I started to live my life anew. Every morning, I gathered plants and herbs, drying and sorting them. Meg Wetherby had made her living selling plants, and I would do the same. I'd arranged with Farmer Johnson to buy some ewes with lambs at foot with my gold coins, and I had a feeling they'd be known to me already. They would provide milk for me and Joseph, and wool to sell. For meat, I'd fish and catch rabbits and pigeons. Ours would not be an easy life, but we were alive.

Gyb had survived my time in North Gate Gaol and now I tucked the wooden toy into my son's hand. It was made for me by his great-grandfather, to bring me comfort on the long journey to the New World. It had brought me comfort down the years, only my journey had been very different to the one Bill Verger had in mind when he'd whittled the wooden cat. Now Gyb would comfort my son as he made his way through life.

The cottage was quiet apart from gurgles and cries, the occasional bark from Barebones, and the icy wind trying to force its way into our home. In the main, we lived in silence. Children needed music and laughter, so I walked in the woods daily, with the collie at heel and the bairn swaddled to my chest, and spoke to him of everything I saw, so he'd hear my voice. Together, we listened to the birds singing as the bare branches around us showed the first signs of green.

I touched the black tips of an ash tree. 'Joseph, see how it's still hung with bunches of ash keys? They'll blow away on the wind and become ash trees themselves one day.'

I bent to kiss the top of his head. One day, I'd blow away and Joseph would have to fend for himself. My chest had weakened from the damp gaol, and I feared that day might not be too far off.

Till that day came, I'd dedicate myself to preparing Joseph for life without me, to finding him a position and another family. I leant against the ash tree and caught my breath. It wasn't wise for me to be outside in this cold but I wanted my son to feel the golden sun on his lovely face and to see the blue sky.

Life was lonely in many ways, but Joseph contained my family within him. In my arms, I held my mother and her mother, and even though I knew very little of them, I'd come to know them through my son.

I stood by the river and watched it for a while. Water was eternal and man was not. Although my arms were filled with new life, I wouldn't last forever and neither would my son. But the water would keep rushing endlessly onwards until it met a bigger river and made its way at last to the open sea. It was enough.

Also by Helen Steadman

If you'd like to find out what becomes of Joseph Leaton, you'll find him alive and well and living in Shotley Bridge in *The Running Wolf*.

The Running Wolf (Shotley Bridge Swordmakers)

The running wolf inscription tells the world that a Solingen blade is at its throat.

Hermann Mohll is a master sword maker from Solingen in Germany who risks his life by breaking his guild oaths and settling in England. While trying to save his family and neighbours from poverty, he is caught smuggling swords and finds himself in Morpeth Gaol facing charges of High Treason.

Determined to hold his tongue and his nerve, Mohll finds himself at the mercy of the corrupt keeper, Robert Tipstaff. The keeper fancies he can persuade the truth out of Mohll and make him face the ultimate justice: hanging, drawing and quartering. But in this tangled web of secrets and lies, just who is telling the truth?

Widdershins (Newcastle Witch Trials Book 1)

England, 1649. Jane Chandler is an apprentice healer. From childhood, she and her mother have used herbs to cure the sick. But Jane will soon learn that her sheltered life in a small village is not safe from the troubles of the wider world.

From his father's beatings to his uncle's raging sermons, John Sharpe is beset by bad fortune. Fighting through personal tragedy, he finds his purpose: to become a witchfinder and save innocents from the scourge of witchcraft.

Widdershins tells the story of the women who were persecuted and the men who condemned them. Based on the little-known

Newcastle witch trials, where fifteen women and one man were hanged for witchcraft on a single day in August 1650.

Sunwise (Newcastle Witch Trials Book 2)

England, 1650. When Jane's lover, Tom, returns from the navy to find her unhappily married to his betrayer, Jane is caught in an impossible situation.

Still reeling from the loss of her mother at the hands of the witchfinder, Jane has no choice but to continue her dangerous work as a healer while keeping her young daughter safe.

But as Tom searches for a way for him and Jane to be together, the witchfinder is still at large.

Filled with vengeance, the witchfinder will stop at nothing in his quest to rid England of the scourge of witchcraft.

God Of Fire (A Greek Myth Retelling)

Repulsed by her ugly newborn, Hera throws him into the sea, where he shatters his ankle. As darkness looms, Thetis saves the wounded child and raises him in her underwater grotto.

Hephaestus is the only Olympian whose injuries never heal, and Zeus adds to his burden by sentencing him to life with Aphrodite. Unhappily married to the adulterous goddess of love, he is fated to repeat his childhood pattern of rejection. To subdue his emotional and physical pain, he harnesses fire to make magical inventions.

Of course, the other gods take advantage of his good nature and demand all manner of trinkets. But the god of fire is nobody's fool. His magic has a shadow side, as gods and mortals learn to their cost when Zeus orders him to create Pandora's jar.

AUTHOR NEWSLETTER

For updates and news about Helen's books, please sign up to her author newsletter at helensteadman.com.

Acknowledgements

When I started researching witches way back in 2011, I came upon a number of local witch trials. In 1673, in nearby Riding Mill, a young girl accused her neighbours of witchcraft, which led to some of the strangest confessions in the history of witch trials. In the end, I decided to base *Widdershins* on the Newcastle witches, but I often considered writing about these curious trials.

I'd been interested for a while in telling Rose's story, and she and her son appear in *The Running Wolf*. So I knew Rose and Joseph had a future, and what happened to them in it, but there was a blur between the end of *Sunwise* and the start of *The Running Wolf*. I had it in mind to tell the strange story of the Riding Mill witch trials, and in one of many early drafts of *Solstice*, that's exactly what happened. Thirteen Mutton Cloggers found themselves on trial for misdemeanours dreamt up by a young woman with too much time on her hands. But as time wore on, I released them one by one. Then I had a story I was broadly happy with, told through the dual perspectives of Rose Driver and Tom Verger. The cover was designed. The book was ready to send to the developmental editor. Then I had a last-minute change of heart and decided it just wasn't right. The story needed to be told from Patience Leaton's point of view. So Tom was ousted and Patience made it onto the cover.

Even though I veered away from telling the story of the Riding Mill trials, it is very much worth your while reading about them. If you look on my website at helensteadman.com you'll find some information about them (assuming I haven't broken my blog again).

Heartfelt thanks must go to those who did the heavy lifting, especially to Julian Webb, developmental editor, who has accompanied me on the journey through the Widdershins Trilogy. (Any mistakes are of course entirely my own, and I apologise heartily for them in advance.)

Just like its elder sisters, *Solstice* is a beautifully dressed book, thanks to Ollie Eskriett of Move Design, who designed not one but two covers for *Solstice*, and I am especially grateful to him for replacing Tom with Patience at the eleventh hour. (Because all the best trilogies have three-and-a-half books in them, Ollie is storing Tom safely on a digital shelf in case I dust him down one day and let him tell the tale of his time aboard *The Durham*.)

In the meantime, thank you to all the lovely bloggers, readers, reviewers and booksellers who have been so supportive of me and my Mutton Clog chronicles.

Finally, those of you who wonder whether it's a real place will be happy to know that Mutton Clog does exist, not a million miles away from Shotley Bridge, though you might struggle to find it on modern maps...

About the Author

For more information about my books, or to sign up to my author newsletter, please visit helensteadman.com.

Printed in Great Britain
by Amazon